CRESCENT LEGACY

THE CRESCENT WITCH CHRONICLES - BOOK THREE

NICOLE R. TAYLOR

CHAPTER 1

The air was cold, but it wasn't anything new. Ireland was always chilly.

I shivered as I followed Boone through the forest, gingerly stepping over fallen logs and weaving around ancient tree trunks. Mist clung to the open parts of the landscape, and I buried deeper into my leather jacket, nestling my chin into my fluffy black scarf.

My boots slipped on a patch of moss, and I yelped. My legs flew out from underneath me, and I landed flat on my ass with a thud.

"Is it much farther?" I asked, moaning when I felt icy water seep through my jeans.

Boone turned and came back to fetch me. I took his hand, and he hauled me up, not even cracking a smile at my clumsiness.

"We'll be there soon," he replied, his Irish accent sounding thicker than usual.

I nodded and tightened my grip on his hand. This was a difficult thing for me to face, but for Boone, it was so much more. Going back to the very spot he was attacked by one of the higher faes and where Aileen had been swallowed by the earth was painful, to say the least. For so long, he'd believed he was to blame for my mother's death. He'd lived with it for a long time, and now a vision a tree had shown me had led him back. It was all a little wearing on the soul after everything we'd been through.

The vision the ancient hawthorn had shown me had staked the fires of hope so high that the heat was almost unbearable. To think my mother, Aileen, could still be alive and trapped under the earth was startling.

Protecting magic, fighting Carman…I couldn't do it alone. As a shapeshifter, Boone was a creature of magic, but he wasn't like me. To have another Crescent Witch beside me would be amazing, but for it to be the mother I never knew? That was epic.

Boone let my hand go and walked again, leading me through the forest. I studied the back of his head, taking in his messy black hair, the black and red checkered pattern of the shirt collar peeking out from underneath his jacket, and the way his legs pushed through the carpet of emerald ferns. It felt like we were in a funeral procession, not a possible rescue mission.

"Are you still worried about the wolf thing?" I asked, watching him carefully.

Only a day had passed since the ritual that had almost taken my life. The ritual that was supposed to break the curse locking Carman out of Ireland. In a moment of raw agony, Boone had done something neither of us knew he was capable of. He'd shifted into the shape of a wolf—a shape he'd never formed before—and broke through the magic keeping us apart like it was nothing at all.

He had been beautiful. His fur silver and his chest and paws snowy white, but the beast in him had full control.

Seeing Boone like that had been terrifying, to say the least. The only thing that had brought him back had been a touch of Crescent magic.

"Of course, I'm worried about it," he said over his shoulder. "I changed faster than I ever have before, I healed the cuts on your arms with my spit, and I broke through Lucy's magical barrier..." At the mention of Lucy, he grimaced and glanced away.

Remembering the moment his wolf jaws had closed around her throat, I shivered, glad he wasn't looking at me. I had been through something terrible that night, but so had he. I was dealing, but Boone... He wasn't. Not really. He was good at pretending, but I could see right through him like a greasy paper bag.

"I'm sorry, I didn't mean it like that."

"I know." He shrugged. "I was a wolf before. So what?"

I sighed, knowing I wouldn't get anything coherent out of him when he was in a mood. His amnesia was a sore point, *literally*.

Not wanting to give him a magically induced headache, I let it go.

We walked in silence, the mist clinging to the forest dulling all the usual sounds. I used to be afraid of being alone out here, not knowing who was lurking in the shadows, but since I'd discovered I was a Crescent Witch, the vastness of this place felt more like home with every passing day.

My power helped me hear the earth. The whispering of the wind, the bird songs, the rustling of tiny creatures in the underbrush, the unfurling of leaves, the sprouting of seeds. It was quite beautiful in a way. Nature was wild and untamable, and none of us were as alone as we were led to believe.

Ahead, Boone came to a halt, and I stopped beside him.

"Is this it?" I asked, peering into the clearing.

He nodded, his jaw tight. We must've passed the limit of Derrydun's hawthorns some time ago. Here, we were exposed, but it didn't seem like it mattered anymore. At least, not for Boone.

My gazed raked over the clearing. I didn't get it. The ground was smooth. Slow growing moss had grown in between the dew-soaked grass, and a bird happily flitted through the branches overhead. There was no sign of twisted roots or anything else that might've disturbed the earth. Nothing at all.

It hadn't even been a year. Far from it, actually. It stood to reason there would be something here. Some kind of sign there'd been a battle between a witch and a higher fae.

"There's nothing here," I said, edging around the clearing. "Nothing at all."

"I don't understand…" Boone walked into the center of the open space, looking around in shock. "It was here. I'm sure of it." He pointed to a tree opposite to where I was standing. "Right there. That's where she…" He knelt, placing his palms on the earth. "Skye, I…I don't understand. I remember it like it happened yesterday. The look on her face…"

"Stop," I whispered, my voice feeling louder than it should in the silent forest. "There are a lot of things I don't understand about this world, but there's one thing that's pretty darn universal. Death."

Boone glanced up at me, his almost-black eyes shining mysteriously. I couldn't look at him, so I turned away.

"Skye, wait."

I hesitated, hugging myself to keep warm.

"You're not goin' to try to sense anythin'? If you try, I'm sure you might find somethin'."

He was so desperate to believe Aileen was still alive that it broke my heart. After all these years believing he was to blame for her death, to have his hope taken away... I sighed and turned toward him.

"I can't feel anything," I said with a shrug. "It's just a forest, Boone. Trees, grass, ferns. There's a deer somewhere close and a couple of birds. A frog. Maybe it's a toad. I don't know the difference. Aileen isn't here."

"The hawthorn led you here for a reason."

I shrugged, starting to believe I'd misread the vision.

"Put your hands on the ground," he said. "*Please.*"

"I'd know if she were here."

"*Please.*"

I sucked in a deep breath and sank to my knees before him. If it finally put his mind to rest, then I would do it even though I already knew what I would find.

Winding my fingers through the grass, I set my palms on the earth. The air was full of the damp scent of dirt, grass, and fresh rain. Mud and dew seeped through the knees of my jeans as I allowed my magic to flow.

It trickled from the pit of my stomach and along all my nerve endings, tingling like I had a bad case of pins and needles. When my senses filtered through the top layer of dirt, I tensed and closed my eyes, aware Boone was watching me closely.

I delved deeper, passing a worm, a rock, and more dirt...but there was no sign of the unnatural roots of a spriggan, only the thick tendrils of the oak forest and the fine web of ferns around us. There were no bones. No remains. Nothing.

When I'd killed the fae that had stolen the face of my ex-boyfriend, Alex, he'd dissolved into ash and blew away on the wind. Hannah had probably wound up the same, but it didn't account for Aileen. I would still feel some kind of trace. An echo. A ghostly tendril. A sprinkle of Crescent magic. *Her bones…*

Holding onto my sigh, I went as deep as I dared, but my search was fruitless. It was the same feeling I'd had when I'd tried to find Aileen in her coffin. She wasn't here.

I opened my eyes, my shoulders sinking as my magic subsided. Glancing at Boone, our eyes met, and he knew.

"No…" he whispered. "I can't believe…"

Standing, I cupped his cheek, my skin rasping on his stubble. "I'm sorry, Boone. I wanted her to be here, too. I really did. Maybe the hawthorn was trying to tell me something else. I'm beginning to understand symbols aren't so literal in this world."

"I thought…"

I wrapped my arms around his neck and held him close.

"Me, too," I whispered. "Me, too."

When we got back to the cottage, the light was already fading. It was totally weird how early it got dark here. Boone said the sun set as early as four p.m. in the middle of winter. I knew it was going to mess with my equilibrium, not to mention my sleeping patterns.

Speaking of Boone… I let him go on ahead, hanging back when I saw the light on in the garden shed. He was so lost in his thoughts, he hadn't noticed, but he needn't worry. Nothing evil was lurking among the rakes and shovels. One almost transparent wisp of magic told me it was just the demon child who'd taken up residence in my spare bedroom, otherwise known as the goth girl Mairead, doing God knew what.

Crossing the lawn, I readied myself for anything. I hadn't taken her for having a green thumb, so either she had a crop of hydroponically grown marijuana or she… Well, I had no bloody idea, so I was going with the weed as the likely explanation.

Peering through the door, I raised my eyebrows when I saw her sitting on a wooden crate in front of a large canvas with a bag of paints at her feet and a mason jar full of murky water and assorted brushes. I didn't know whether to be proud or disappointed.

Stepping into the shed, I shivered. How she could stand the cold was beyond my little Australian mind. I was used to blistering summers and mild winters. Snow sometimes happened back home but only for a second, and it never stuck around long enough for a snowball fight.

"Where have you been?" Mairead asked, glancing up from her canvas.

"Just went for a walk with Boone," I replied, not wanting to disappoint her with my fruitless search for Aileen. "Quality time, you know. What's all this about?" I nodded at the palette of paint in her lap. "You've got green on your face."

"*Cac*, have I?" She swiped the back of her hand across her cheek, making the dob of paint smear even more.

"What are you painting?" I rounded the canvas and took in the image. It was a mess of green splotches and didn't really resemble anything. "Is it abstract?"

"No. It's supposed to be a landscape." She made a face

and pointed to the picture sticky taped to the makeshift easel she'd constructed out of old boxes.

Narrowing my eyes, I studied the image she'd likely printed out at Irish Moon and nodded. It was Derrydun from a distance. The main road stretched across the picture, giving a great view of all the shops. There was Molly McCreedy's, the bright pink of Mary's Teahouse, Irish Moon was there, and in the center of the street was the hawthorn. Further afield, I could see the ruined tower house on the horizon and the forest surrounding the sleepy village.

"That's supposed to be that?" I asked, pointing to the canvas.

"I'm workin' on it," she replied with a pout. "I watched a video on the Internet where they were dabbin' all the colors on like this…" She slapped the brush against the canvas, adding more green to the shape she'd already created. "Buildin' color."

"What's that green thing supposed to be?" I asked, tilting my head to the side.

"That part's the hill."

"Really?"

"*Skye!*"

I laughed, feeling a little lighter after mine and Boone's emotional bender in the woods.

"Are you feelin' okay?" Mairead asked, her brush falling into the jar of water with a *plop*.

"Fine," I replied, rubbing my arms. The gashes from the ritual had almost faded—all that was left were two pale pink lines—but it was more nervous energy that forced me to rub than any pain.

Mairead didn't look convinced.

"Do you want to go inside?" I asked. "My nipples feel

like they'll get frostbite and drop off. Anyway, I promised I'd look at your drawings and help you figure out shit. I kinda got waylaid the other night."

"You had an excuse." She glanced at my arm, worried Boone's weird tongue magic was going to reverse itself, and I would bleed out on the spot.

"Don't worry about it," I said. "I'm not going to explode, you know."

"You're not worried about it," she argued. "You're not angry, or sad, or anythin'. You're just…*meh*."

I shrugged. I kinda was, but wallowing got no one anywhere. Man, when did I start growing up? I was being all wise and shit. Maybe Boone was rubbing off on me. Not in the literal sense, because we rubbed off on one another all the time, but in the philosophical kind of way.

Thinking about Lucy and the Nightshade witches, the ritual that was supposed to kill me and let Carman back into Ireland, the mass burning of the family I'd never met, the hatred toward my coven for standing up to Carman a thousand years ago, how they were ostracized for closing the doorways to the fae realm to stop a war from breaking out, and all the other injustices that had led to the Crescents calling me home, I scowled. I suppose I was angry. Real angry.

"But—"

"Life has to go on, Mairead," I interrupted. "We're fine, but we still have to do our duty by Derrydun. Boone and I… We can't take a day off from that. We've just gotta deal and get on with it."

"Not even after…" Her bottom lip trembled.

"Not even after near-death experiences. The bad guys won't take time off for a weekend at the seaside, so neither can we. They'll keep trying, and we have to be there to keep stopping them."

"It's not fair."

I smiled and wrapped my arm around her shoulder. "It never is."

Leaning against the kitchen table, I watched Boone as he sliced some carrots, tilting my head to the side.

He had a really nice ass. Firm, round, and just—

"What are you lookin' at?" he asked, not even turning around.

"How do you know I'm looking at you?" I retorted, leaning back in the chair, forgetting about the studying I was supposed to be doing. The Crescent spell book was before me, open at random page talking about magical Legacy—the word *Legacy* capitalized like it was a thing I was supposed to know—while Boone did what he did best. Cook for me.

"Do we really need to keep havin' this conversation?" he asked, dumping the chopped carrots into a huge silver pot on the stove.

"No." I sighed and shook my head. Boone always knew when I was staring at his ass. *Always.* I figured it was a magical animal thing, and animals were all into the 'deed.' You know, the *nasty*. He was a man, after all. "I thought you'd like me staring at your juicy peach."

He turned, his brow furrowed. "Juicy peach?"

"Moneymaker?" I offered.

His lips twitched into a ghost of a smile before he turned around and resumed chopping, this time, starting on the potatoes.

A week after the ritual, and Boone was still fretting. His facial expression hadn't changed from brooding—which was one of two settings he had, the other being cocky—and it was really beginning to worry me. At least, this time, he'd been transparent about it rather than hiding his fears away and stewing in his own juices. We all knew what happened last time he did that. Well, it did end up with us having sex in a ditch in the middle of the forest, but I couldn't count on that happening again. While I liked being adventurous, I would rather my bare ass lay on something a little less…*rocky*.

"Where's Mairead?" Boone asked over his shoulder.

"In the shed again."

"Paintin'?"

"I should probably get her a heater," I mused. "Or a hot-water bottle. It's a pity I can't spell her a fire pit or something." It was a cool idea, but something like that would be a flare for wandering fae and craglorn. I may as well put up a flashing neon sign that said, All You Can Eat Buffet Now Open.

Rolling my eyes, I glanced down at my arms and shoved up my sleeves. When I'd jumped into the shower that morning, I'd been shocked to find the little pink scars had vanished. They were gone, kaput, erased, gone like they'd never been there at all. Magic wolf spit, indeed.

Turning back to the spell book, I flipped over the page. In all the time I'd been rifling through the ancient book I'd found under the floorboards, I couldn't remember seeing anything about shape-shifting wolves that could heal with their tongues. There wasn't anything about the Nightshade Witches or any other coven for that matter.

As per usual, I was flying blind and fumbling in the dark, and all the other clever sayings for being a clueless biatch I could think of.

I turned the page again and paused when I saw a hand-drawn picture of a nightshade flower. It was just an explanation of the plant and its various properties, but it felt like a sign. The entire magical world was all about omens. I'd had enough flashed in my face to last a lifetime, so I figured I had a good inbuilt omen detector by now. Maybe this was one I should be listening to.

Thinking about the night of the ritual, I winced as I felt the phantom pain of Lucy's dagger slicing my arms. The blade had cut from elbow to wrist, severing veins and parting flesh and muscle. The amount of blood pouring from me onto the ground had been horrific.

Shaking my head, I pushed the memory away. Just thinking about it made me want to hurl.

Lucy said Carman had her family and were using them as leverage for her to perform the ritual. Now that it was all over, what had happened to her mother, grandmother, and fifteen-year-old sister? Had Carman let them go? Doubtful. Had she even taken them in the first place? Carman couldn't get into Ireland, but it didn't mean much. She'd had her thugs snatch Mairead off the street in Dublin, so the same could've happened to the Nightshade Witches.

But if they were free and they found out Boone took Lucy out to save me, then we would likely have a bunch of evil witches who were out for revenge to add to the pile of problems we already had. Witches who'd had their magic taken by Aileen, but... *Hang on.* Lucy *and* her sister had been spared. They'd been given a chance to redeem their coven, but look at what happened.

Glancing at the sketch, I ran my fingers over the lines of ink, tracing the outline of the flower. *Lucy's sister...*

Where did Lucy say she was from? Galway. Where was that? I had a copy of her resume with her home address. Maybe I could wrangle a loan of Sean McKinnon's little red Toyota Corolla again so I could go and check. Just to be on the safe side. It was about the only proactive thing— other than standing guard over Derrydun and the ancient hawthorn, aka the ultimate doorway to another plane of existence—I could do.

Glancing at Boone, I blurted, "Hey, do you think you could convince Sean to lend me his car again?"

He raised his eyebrows. "After last time? You'd have a better chance of spellin' Mrs. Boyle's broomstick...if you can pry it from her fingers."

I snorted, remembering our trip to Croagh Patrick. On the way back, we'd been soaked to the bone by a flurry of hungry sluagh who'd tried to drown me in the spring. Cue drenched upholstery and muddy floors. Sean wasn't pleased, and Boone had spent an entire afternoon sucking out the muck from the interior with a wet and dry vacuum cleaner in an attempt to win back his mate.

"It's important."

"I can ask," he said, tipping the last of the vegetables into the pot. "But I can't make any promises."

"Thanks."

"Where are you goin'?" He put the lid on the pot and sat across from me, a concerned look on his face.

I glanced at the spell book again. If I found them there, what would I do?

"Skye… You're not goin' to find the Nightshade Witches are you?"

"So what if I am?" I snapped, closing the spell book.

He pinched the bridge of his nose. "Are you goin' to kill them?"

His words were blunt and direct and hit me right where it hurt.

"I don't want to, but what if I have to?"

"Skye, you don't—"

"There are lots of things I don't want to do," I interrupted, knowing I was being a little insensitive to the fact he'd killed Lucy. Our situation had always been life and death, but facing the actual dying part wasn't sunshine and rainbows. "But I have to do them; otherwise…" Resting my elbows on the table, I fisted my hands in my hair. "They murdered my family. They tried to murder me. She tried to murder you. How am I supposed to react to that? With lollypops and marshmallows and puppies and kittens?"

"I didn't say—"

"I'm going to Galway, and I'm going to find out what happened to them. I'm going to find out the truth." I straightened up and eyeballed Boone.

"And if you don't like what you find?"

I curled my hands into tight fists, struggling to keep my anger in check. "Then I'll do what I have to do to protect magic from those that would destroy it. If it's taken from us, there will be nothing to protect the world from Carman and what lies on the other side of those doorways."

Boone nodded, his expression solemn. "Do you want me to come with you?"

"No. I have to do this alone."

"Are you sure?"

"Yes. This is Crescent business. This part, I have to do on my own."

He sighed, then glanced at the stove as the stew inside began to bubble. "Then I'll ask Sean tomorrow."

Standing out the front of Irish Moon, I pulled down my beanie over my ears and blew out a plume of vaporized breath. Man, it was cold. Just like my mood.

"You can wait inside, you know," Mairead said, poking her head out the door.

"I know, but I've got ants in my pants." I shifted my weight from foot to foot, then shoved my hands inside my jacket and wedged them under my armpits for warmth. "Besides, you just want me to help you rearrange the bookcases."

"It wouldn't hurt. I want to get it finished before openin'."

"Tourist season is winding down," I retorted.

"So?"

Turning back to the street, I resumed my watch. In the distance, I could see the single set of traffic lights shining through the mist and the manufactured glow of the Topaz service station. Beyond that, the landscape melted into milky whiteness. It was all a little creepy if you asked me.

"Still got to keep busy," Mairead added.

"If you say so."

"Where are you goin' anyway?" she asked, still lingering behind me.

I couldn't really tell her I was going on a mission to find and possibly punish some really bad witches, so I gave her a smartass comment instead.

"You're letting out all the warm air," I replied. "I pay for that, you know."

"Buy me a present, okay?" she retorted with a *humph* before retreating inside.

The door slammed closed, the sound strangely muffled by the dense fog.

A pair of headlights broke their way through the mist, and a little red car came into view. It hurtled down the road, through the red traffic light, screeched around the hawthorn, and came to a sudden stop beside me. The door flung open, and Boone got out.

"It's a miracle," I declared as he rounded the bonnet and stood beside me. "How did you convince Sean?"

"Don't ask," Boone drawled, his accent sounding thicker than usual. "I'm goin' to pay for it for a while."

"Your torment is greatly appreciated."

"Are you sure you don't want me to come with you?" he asked, handing me the keys.

I nodded. "I'll be fine. I know a few more things now. It's not like the thing with the craglorn."

Boone grimaced and pulled me in for a hug. "No, it's not. It's worse."

"Stop fretting like an old woman," I complained. "I'll let you know when I'm on the way home."

He smiled and kissed me on the lips.

"What's that for?" I asked.

"What's what for?"

"That cheeky smile."

"I like it when you call Derrydun home."

"Don't make me feel better. This is going to be hard enough as it is."

"There's goin' to be a lot of difficult decisions in the

future," Boone said. "But I know you'll make the right one."

"I suppose." Taking the keys, I kissed him on the lips. "Be careful."

"Don't worry about me," I said, spreading my arms out wide. "I'm a badass, remember?"

Sliding into the driver's seat, I hooked up my mobile phone onto the dashboard and plugged in the address on Google Maps. I gave Boone one last wave as I started up Sean's Toyota Corolla and tore off down the road. The sooner I was there, the sooner I could be on my way back.

It wasn't long before the little car broke through the low-lying mist. Derrydun sat in a hollow, so while the world went on in the sunshine, the weather clung to the little valley like glue.

Following the directions the robotic voice spat out at me, I turned onto a highway, and then a smaller road before it narrowed into an alarmingly small stretch that had me on edge. There wasn't much room for oncoming traffic to pass. If I edged a little too far to the side, I would write off Sean's car, and then I would be in the *cac* big time. At least nothing was coming the other way.

I spoke too soon.

Rounding a bend, I yelped as I saw a giant truck hurtling toward me. My eyes widened and a cold sweat prickled across my forehead. *I wasn't going to make it!*

I let out a wail as the lorry blasted its horn, passing by so close I could almost smell the driver's armpits. It receded into the distance, leaving me shaken.

"Where the hell are you taking me?" I screamed at the map. "This place is a deathtrap!"

The little red car coasted, and finally, the road opened up, giving me some breathing space. I knew this place was absolutely bonkers, but driving in this country was like performing a death-defying stunt. All that was missing were the pyrotechnics.

Ahead, a brown and white sign appeared on the side of the road. It read, *Failte go Co. na Gaillimhe*. Welcome to County Galway. At least I was almost there.

At least… It was becoming my favorite sentence add-on lately. At least, like it could be worse. Well, it could be, but I didn't like having to choose the lesser of two evils. I would rather not choose at all, to be honest.

The countryside flashed by, morphing into small villages, then back to wide open greenery before the outer limits of the city of Galway began to take hold. I knew the town sat on the coast, but I wouldn't have time to visit the seaside or do any souvenir shopping in the center. Cod and chips with a side of Guinness merchandise were not on today's menu.

Bypassing the city center, the map took me across a river and into a more modern residential area. Twisting and turning through the warren of streets, I came to a stop down the street from the address Lucy had given on her resume. I turned off the engine and listened to it clicking as it cooled in the chilly autumn air.

Thanks to Google Street View, I recognized the house at the end of the street. It was white with a russet-colored roof and matching window shutters. A little beige car sat in the stubbly little driveway, and the garden was green and full of lush plants. It was all quaint and normal. Nothing sinister about it at all. I was half expecting a fence made of human skulls and a house comprised of gingerbread and icing.

I didn't know how long I sat there stewing in my own juices. All I had to do was get out of the car, walk up to the front door, and knock. The bit that came after was the mystery. What was waiting for me on the other side? A full-on magical fistfight, or tea and scones?

What a metaphor! I knew another set of doors with exactly the same problem.

Movement caught my attention in the passenger side mirror, and I slid down in the seat. A girl was walking down the footpath, her head down. Earphones were stuck in her ears with the white cord trailing down to her pocket.

She was wearing a school uniform—a green tartan skirt, gray jumper, matching tie, and a forest-green blazer —with a heavy-looking backpack slung sloppily over her shoulder. Her wild blonde curls were pulled back into a ponytail, fixed in place with a black ribbon.

I watched her as she passed, really starting to feel like a creepy pervert. This was what they warned kids about at school. Stranger danger. If it weren't for the fact I could sense what she was, I would've checked myself and turned around before the police knocked on the window.

I snorted. The Nightshade Witches didn't just perform blood rituals, they were into wagging school as well!

The girl—Lucy's sister—walked up to the front door of the house and let herself inside, then the street was empty again.

Now or never.

I got out of the car and strode along the footpath toward the little cottage. Pushing open the gate, I ignored the quaint little garden with its daisies and roses interlaced with nightshade plants and knocked on the door. Footsteps echoed inside, and I tensed, my heart galloping in my chest. That, and I felt like rushing to the loo.

When the door opened, I was surprised to see a woman in her fifties standing on the other side. Curly strawberry-blonde hair, freckled nose, green eyes… It was Lucy's mother.

When she saw me, her expression fell, and she tried to slam the door in my face. I shoved back with my magic, forcing the woman to stumble, and stepped inside the cottage.

"*Christine!*" she shrieked as I advanced.

The moment I crossed the threshold, I could feel traces of Nightshade magic, and I knew… Lucy's family was never kidnapped. They'd never left home at all. It was hard to say if Lucy knew or if she actually believed Carman was holding them. I wanted to say the latter, but it made no difference now. What was done, was done.

The girl rushed out of a room to the side with her hands in the air. Her magic had the bitter taste that Lucy's had the night of the ritual. I threw up my own palms to counter her, and she fell to her knees the moment my power came to life.

An old woman appeared at the end of the hall, her mouth falling open when she saw me standing in the hallway.

"You know who I am," I said. "So you know what I can do."

"*Crescent bitch*," the old woman snarled.

Her words sliced through me, bringing forth the vision the hawthorn had shown me of the burning in the forest. Nightshade Witches had murdered my great-grandmother, my grandmother, and my aunt. I'd heard her say those words before.

"That's right," I said, not liking how this situation was unfolding. "I'm the biggest Crescent bitch of all."

"Lucy… I know what you did to her."

"It didn't have to be this way," I murmured, looking

down on what was left of the Nightshade Witches. "You could've joined me in fighting Carman. I don't want to…"

"All this is your fault," the grandmother said. "All our sufferin' started the moment you severed our connection with the other realm."

I opened my mouth to argue, but it wasn't worth it. I could tell them all about what Carman planned to do. I could tell them the doorways were closed to save them from even more suffering, but I knew they wouldn't listen. They'd made up their minds a long time ago, long before they chose to burn my family at the stake.

"I want to make things right," I said, trying to keep my voice from shaking. "But you took my family away from me. You conspired with the enemy. You were prepared to sacrifice the birthright of *all* the witches of Ireland in the name of petty revenge. You'll never understand true sacrifice." *Sometimes, we had to do terrible things for the greater good to prevail.*

"Who do you think you are?" the mother cried.

"The only witch who's prepared to fight for magic, no matter what," I replied. "Aileen gave you a chance to go on after you murdered our entire family, a chance you didn't deserve. Lucy made her choice when she joined Carman. *You gave up.* You gave your coven to evil. You took the coward's way out. Now I'm here to take your magic away for good. *The greater good.*"

"*No!*" the girl exclaimed. "*Please! You can't take our Legacy!*"

"I'm sorry it had to come to this." I raised my hands and called on my magic. "This is where the Nightshade Witches end. For good this time."

CHAPTER 3

My eyes snapped open, and I sat up, my heart thumping.

The images my dream had conjured up began to fade, and I shoved them away roughly, not wanting to relive them. For once, I was glad I couldn't remember what my brain hallucinated during the night.

Rubbing the grit from my eyes, I sighed. My legs were tangled in the quilt, and I was damp. The sweaty kind of damp, *thank you very much*. My underboob area was particularly moist.

Glancing at the clock, I saw it was five minutes to nine a.m.

"Shoot!" I exclaimed, leaping from the bed. My legs caught in the sheets, and I hurtled toward the floor. Landing on my side, I rolled and sprang to my feet. Holding out my hands, I let out a *whoop*. "An epic save, and no one was around to see it!"

I showered and applied my makeup in a daze, my mind playing over yesterday's confrontation in Galway. It didn't feel good being that person. I wanted people to like me, I wanted to be accepted, and I wanted to belong, but my birthright was an automatic ticket to prejudice.

Yesterday, I'd been the bad guy, and it had sucked bigtime.

Whatever happened next, one thing was certain. Carman had to go. I couldn't banish her, and I couldn't imprison her, so I had to kill her. Gone, finito, kaput. For all time. I couldn't allow anything to get in my way because I would only have one shot.

Shivering, I closed the bathroom door and thudded downstairs to the kitchen. There was a note on the table, handwritten in Comic Sans. It read, *I've gone to open the shop. I demand a raise. Mairead.*

Sighing, I dabbed at my eyes, trying not to smudge my mascara. I asked a lot of that girl, and she jumped, no questions asked. Maybe I should give her a raise. Wait…I gave her free rent, so I should probably play that card first.

I grabbed my jacket from the back of the chair and threw it on as I bolted out the door. Slamming it behind me, I heard the lock click into place, then I legged it across the garden, slipped around the corner like an ice skater, and made for Irish Moon.

The lights were on, casting warm light onto the murky footpath. Opening the door, the little bell jingled as I stepped into the cozy shop. The crystals hummed around me, their energy calming my aura.

Mairead was sitting behind the counter, drawing furiously in a sketchbook. Her long black hair was loose today, and she had on a fluffy black cardigan. Matching black lipstick and eyeliner finished off her classic goth look for the day.

"You were home late last night," she said, not even taking a moment to glance up from her work.

"Yes, Mum," I said with a smirk. "I was."

"Shut up." She made a face. "I was worried about you."

"Smartassery is my way of coping," I said, rounding the counter.

"Where did you go?"

"I just had some stuff to do," I replied with a shrug.

"Magic stuff?" She gave me a pointed look.

Mairead was eighteen, a university drop out, had been disowned by her parents, had only one color in her wardrobe—if you could call black a color—and had been kidnapped by Carman's henchmen. She had enough problems without me dragging her into this world deeper than she already was.

"Just needed to check an item off my to-do list." I flinched internally, trying not to let it show on my face. It was such a callous way of describing the punishment I'd dished out on the Nightshade Witches. And here I was describing myself as the judge, jury, and executioner of all witches when I'd only had my magic unbound... When was it? Not even a year ago.

"What are you drawing?" I changed the subject, not wanting to dwell.

Mairead held up her sketchbook, and I smiled when I saw a rather rough pencil drawing of a fox. It looked rather good. All harsh lines and shading.

"It's meant to be Boone," she said. "I haven't seen him *you know*, so I don't know if he looks like that. I used me imagination."

"It's pretty good."

"Really?"

"Uh-huh." I nodded and ducked under the counter. Rummaging through the pile of papers and assorted junk,

I found the deck of tarot cards all the way at the back. It had been so long since I'd drawn a card that the box felt unfamiliar in my hand.

"Do you think I'll see him change?" she asked, picking up her pencil.

My frown deepened. Boone hadn't shifted since the night of the ritual, and I wasn't sure when he would. I couldn't blame him for hesitating. Having your body practically explode into the shape of a wolf had to put a little fear into you.

"I don't know," I said, opening the box of tarot cards. "It's not a pretty thing to look at. It's quite painful for him, you know."

"Oh…" Her cheeks flushed, and she began scratching her pencil across paper, gouging a deep dent into the page.

"Don't worry about it. There isn't exactly a handbook for these things."

She didn't reply, sinking deeper into her sketch.

Glancing out the window, I began shuffling the cards. The days were getting colder. Soon, the tourist season would be over, and the huge coaches packed with cashed-up holidaymakers would stop until March. I wondered what that would mean for Irish Moon. Should I reduce the opening hours or close for the winter? What would Aileen do?

"Hey," I said. "What happens around here in winter?"

"We freeze our tits off," Mairead replied sullenly.

"Stop being so sensitive," I retorted. "I'm talking about the shop."

"We'd close from Sunday to Tuesday. A couple of backpacker buses come sometimes, but not really. People usually stick to Dublin or Belfast."

Shuffling the cards again, I thought about it. Trying to

keep Irish Moon running and battle an ancient witch hell-bent on destroying magic so she could get to a parallel universe was a major juggling act. I wondered what the cards said about it.

I drew a black and gold rectangle from the center of the deck. Setting the card on the counter, I turned it over, revealing the image was upside down. In the center was a figure in armor with angel wings, sitting in a chariot pulled by two horses. The Chariot.

"Does it mean somethin' different when it's the wrong way around?" Mairead asked, peering over my shoulder.

"I guess so."

Rounding the counter, I went over to the bookcase and scowled when I saw the section on tarot had disappeared. That was right. Mairead had rearranged yesterday.

"I can't find anything anymore," I complained. "What did you do?"

"Stop your sookin'. Tarot is to the left, halfway up. They sell better when they're at eye height."

"Are you sure you want to get into art? Visual merchandising could be a thing."

"I'm sure it's a thing, but I don't want to do visual merchandising."

I raised my eyebrows. "What's this then?"

"Boredom."

Rolling my eyes, I found the section on tarot and pulled out a book. I flipped through, studying the contents page. Not finding what I was looking for, I took down another and found a section on reversals.

"Great," I muttered. "Back to front means doom and gloom."

"A turned over horse and cart doesn't sound good, anyway."

Finding a page on the Chariot, I scanned the interpretation and mulled over it. Two stubborn forces going head-to-head. No one is prepared to back down and would go at it until the other fell.

Basically, it was game on. A fight to the death was looming, which wasn't anything I didn't already know, but now it was showing up in the cards. After all this time looming across the horizon, it was finally going to happen…and soon.

"What does it mean?" Mairead asked.

"Game on…"

Tossing the book away, I grabbed the laptop from the back room and fired it up.

"What are you doing?" Mairead asked, her sketchbook forgotten.

"Looking at the news," I replied, setting the computer on the counter.

"Why?"

"*Shh,*" I hissed, scrolling through the Irish Times website. "*Noo…*"

Among all the stories about politics, complaining about politics, the latest social media craze, and assorted stories on new obscure research findings—*boys twice as likely to cheat on exams*—was a story on a strange crop blight.

That was how it began last time. At least, it did in the stories. Carman and her sons laid waste to Ireland, killing crops and spreading disease wherever they went.

Did I really have to die for the curse to be broken? Maybe my blood was enough. If that were the case, then Ireland was completely open for the taking. Carman could already be here!

"What's the dirtiest word you know in Irish?" I asked,

starting to walk anxious laps around the display of tumbled stones.

"Uh..."

"How do you say the f-word?"

"There isn't really a way of sayin' that in Irish... There is the c-word."

"Even I get scandalized when someone says the c-word." I fisted my hands in the tub of polished amethyst and tried to absorb the calming energy.

"You, scandalized?"

"The c-word is forbidden, Mairead! *Forbidden!*"

"You could say *gabh transna ort fhéin.*"

"What's that mean?"

"Go...you know...yourself sideways. Pretty much, anyway."

"*Gabh transna... ort fhéin...*" The words sounded strange on my tongue but were oddly satisfying to shout out. "*Gabh transna ort fhéin!*"

A blast of cold air buffeted me as the door opened, and I wrenched my hands from the tumbled stones, sending some clattering to the floor.

"I hope you're not sayin' that to me," Boone said, wiping his boots on the mat.

"Thank goodness you're here," Mairead exclaimed, venturing out from behind the counter so she could scoop up the amethyst. "Skye's gone insane."

I snatched up the tarot card and shoved it at him. "Look!"

"The Chariot?"

"It's upside down!" I said, flailing my arms.

"Skye says it's doom and gloom," Mairead said, her voice echoing from behind the display.

I raised my eyebrows and widened my eyes, nodding at Mairead. Boone made a face and took out his wallet.

"Here's a fiver," he said, handing Mairead the money. "Go over to Mary's, and get a coffee or somethin'."

"I'm not a kid, you know." She pouted but snatched the money from his fingers anyway.

"I know you're not, but do you want to deal with that?" He gestured toward me.

"Hey!" I cried. "I'm standing right here!"

Mairead took my outburst as her cue to make a run for it. Bolting for the door, she pushed outside and hurtled across the street toward Mary's Teahouse.

"Don't be so hard on her. She just wants to be included," Boone said, rubbing his palm up and down my arm.

"I know, but she's human. She doesn't have anything to protect herself with."

"She handled herself just fine when…" He hesitated.

"She got lucky." I picked up a piece of amethyst from the floor and tossed it back into the tub with the others. "The talisman protected her in the end, but it's what got her kidnapped in the first place."

"What's wrong?"

"*Everything.*" Turning the laptop around, I pointed to the screen.

Boone narrowed his eyes and read the headline.

"A crop blight?" he asked, clearly not getting it.

"It's Carman," I said. "This was how it started last time. The crops failed all over Ireland, then people started getting sick."

"There's no way to link that to Carman," he argued. "It's just one crop. Besides, I stopped the ritual remember?"

I grimaced and fell silent.

"Skye…"

"Did you?" I asked. "Did you really stop it?"

Boone didn't reply, but he started to look rather worried. He wasn't sure, either.

"She's not going to come straight at me," I went on. "She'll gather her strength, suck the magic out of everything she can get her hands on, and when she's had her fill, she'll come for the hawthorn."

"The hawthorn in the forest?"

"That's where it all started. That's where my ancestors sealed the doorways. She's coming here."

"Maybe, but there's no way of knowin' this story is linked to Carman," he said, pointing at the laptop. "There's no way of knowin' anythin'."

"Then what about the Chariot?"

"I think you need to calm down," he murmured. "I can feel you…"

I raised my eyebrows and felt the tension in my shoulders. Placing my hand on my stomach, I sensed my magic simmering just beneath the surface.

"Oh…" This instinctual business was wreaking havoc when my emotions went haywire. I hadn't noticed it before, even when my monthly lady time came to visit, but my magic was growing every day. PMS was going to be a real barrel of *craic*.

Boone's arms curled around me, and he pulled me against his chest. Holding me tightly, he soothed my anxiety until the golden light dulled.

"Can you keep cuddling me forever?" I asked. "Just like this?"

His chest rose as he breathed in deeply, and I nestled closer. What would I do without him? I'd be lost.

"We don't know anythin' for sure," he said after a moment. "Worryin' about things we can't control won't get us anywhere. We've got some time to figure it out."

"The cards are warning us."

"Aye. So we can be vigilant."

"You're so smart."

Boone laughed, and it was a sweet sound to my ears. Despite all of his own problems—his amnesia, his crazy wolf shape, and his new magic-nullifying abilities—he still found it in himself to calm me down with his Yoda-esque wisdom.

"I'm sorry," I whispered.

"We're goin' through tough times," Boone replied. "And I made a promise to you and Aileen. We may have lost her, but we're still here. And while we're still breathin'…"

"We keep fighting."

"Aye."

"Something Carman said is still bothering me," I murmured.

"What?"

"It was like she expected to see someone else."

She hasn't come forth… I worried the words in my mind, trying to understand the meaning. Reincarnation? No, that was absurd even after all the weird things Boone and I had seen. Maybe she expected a link to the hawthorns? They had forced memories into my mind. It was possible Carman expected the tree to link me to the Crescent who'd cursed her and closed the way to the fae realm. I was the last of my coven. It stood to reason…but the hawthorn hadn't linked me to anything.

"Maybe she expected to be facin' Aileen."

"Maybe…"

Peering over his shoulder, I caught sight of Mairead coming out of Mary's with a paper bag in her hand. *Those better be cookies…*

"Are you feelin' a bit better?" Boone asked, sensing her approach.

I nodded as he let me go. "For now. Will you come over tonight?"

"Aye," he said. "I wanted to ask for your help."

"With?"

He frowned and shrugged. "With me wolf shape…"

"Oh…" My heart twisted as the door opened.

"Is it safe?" Mairead called out. "I brought cookies. *Chocolate ones.*"

"*Outta my way!*" I exclaimed shoving Boone aside.

"You've got a real problem with sugar," he said, shaking his head. "A real problem."

CHAPTER 4

The memory of Boone's wolf shape haunted my thoughts for the rest of the day.

The white and silver of his coat were beautiful, but his snapping jaws and burning eyes were a stark reminder of the beast hidden underneath the sweet Irishman I'd come to love. Who knew what kind of person he'd been before his memory had been taken?

It didn't matter. Who he was now was more important to him than what he'd been before. Besides, a person's core didn't change when you took away their memories.

After locking up Irish Moon, Mairead went off to work on her painting, and I went over to Molly McCreedy's.

I crossed the street, passing under the hawthorn tree as I went. Her branches tickled the top of my head, spreading warmth through my frosty fingers. Old Fergus's donkey was tied up out the front of the pub, her nose in a feedbag. Her big brown eyes found mine as I approached, and her ears flicked forward.

"Hey, girl," I murmured, rubbing the swirl of chestnut

hair between her eyes. "Fergus doesn't go anywhere without you, does he?"

The donkey lowered her head and resumed eating, the promise of food better value than talking to me. Leaving her to the bliss her oats were giving her, I pushed into the pub.

Maggie was pulling a beer when I approached the bar. Sitting on my usual stool, I peered out the back and saw Boone elbows deep in the sink, scrubbing a large cast-iron pot. With all the troubles we'd had lately, it was a rather normal thing to be doing. I hated doing the dishes, but it was strange how even the most mundane tasks had become cherished items on the to-do list in the wake of having my arms sliced from wrist to elbow.

Maggie let out a loud laugh at old Fergus, who'd told her one of his dirty jokes by the sounds of it. His Jack Russell terrier was sitting under his feet, curled up on the floorboards and never made a peep.

Thankfully, Sean McKinnon hadn't arrived for his nightly vigil over a pint glass, so I was spared his smartass commentary. For tonight at least.

"Skye," Maggie said, leaning against the bar when she was done. "Where's your kid?"

I scowled. "She's not my kid."

"I'm just jokin'. Calm your farm. It's a good thing what you've done for her."

"Tell that to her parents." I rolled my eyes. "I saw Beth at the Topaz yesterday, and she looked at me like I was possessed with the devil or something. I was surprised she didn't cross herself before she ran away."

"With a daughter like Mairead? I can't believe it." She clucked her tongue. "If Mairead wasn't happy at Trinity, then she wasn't happy. Best she finds out now than in three years when it's time to start repayin' the student loans."

"That's a good point."

"Did you go to university back in Australia?"

I nodded. "I did a Bachelor of Arts."

Maggie laughed, her eyes sparkling. "The most useless degree in the world."

"You don't have to tell me that. Life works in mysterious ways. Mairead tells me she wants to be an artist."

"Really?" The barmaid's ears pricked up. "Is she any good? Maybe she can paint us a new portrait of Molly McCreedy."

I glanced at the painting hanging over the open fireplace. "That one? It's an original, isn't it?"

"An original paint by numbers from the Internet." Maggie winked.

I gasped dramatically. "Are you saying there's no such thing as a Molly McCreedy?"

She tapped her nose. "Mum's the word."

"*Nooo…*"

"The tourists love the story," she said. "The pub's as old as the hills, but Molly McCreedy was just a name they made up. There was never any Molly. No one ever told you?"

"The whole village knows? Why didn't anyone tell me!"

"Well, you were new even though your mam was Aileen. Then they probably figured Boone'd tell you."

"I'm shattered. Absolutely shattered."

Maggie nodded toward the taps of beer. "Can I get you somethin' to drink to soothe your broken heart?"

"Nah. I'm waiting for Boone."

"We'll let him go in a few," she said. "How've you been keepin'? You haven't been around in a while."

"I've been busy, I guess," I said with a shrug. I couldn't exactly tell her about the time I almost became a human sacrifice, so busy it was. "Tourist season is winding down, and I've been trying to figure out how to keep things going over the winter." It was a half-truth but the truth nonetheless.

"It does get quiet here over the chilly months, to be sure. Aileen used to have shortened openin' hours and close down over the Christmas and New Year holidays."

"Mairead said."

"Hey, have you thought about openin' an online shop? There's good money in the Internet."

"The thought has crossed my mind…" But now I knew why Aileen never did. The whole Crescent thing was time-consuming, to say the least.

"Hey," Boone said as he walked out of the kitchen. "You're early."

"Can't keep my main man waiting," I said with a smile.

He leaned over the bar and gave me a kiss, lingering a little too long for Maggie's taste.

"*Eww*," she declared. "Get out of here, and take your sickly sweet lovey-dovey talk with you." She flicked Boone with a tea towel as he darted around the end of the bar.

He grabbed my hand and dragged me from the stool, and we made a quick getaway, the old boozehounds of Derrydun bellowing with laughter as we went.

It was already dark outside by the time we approached the hawthorn in the forest. Overhead, a fine layer of clouds obscured the stars, and the moon was a waxing crescent. The night was almost absolute as we walked along the well-worn path into the forest. The way was familiar, even though I couldn't see it very well, and I felt the presence of the ancient hawthorn long before I laid eyes on it.

It was always like that, though. The more in tune I became with my magic, the easier it was to sense what was around me. I could even sense Boone across Derrydun if he were tapping into his shapeshifter-ness. Was this how Aileen had felt? I wished she were here so I could ask. It was a little bittersweet in the aftermath of last week's misadventures.

The hawthorn loomed before us as we stepped out into the clearing, its branches stretching over us. I sensed the power in its leaves and was glad for its protection. Hawthorns guarded words and magic, so whatever we did tonight would be a private affair.

"I should've brought a torch," Boone said, his voice loud in the silence.

"I have something a little better than a torch," I murmured, holding up my hand.

Focusing, I worked my magic down my arm and into my fingers, fashioning a little ball of golden light in my palm. Willing it to hover, I sent it into the air. It spun and glowed brightly as I stepped back. It looked like a firefly as it began wandering the clearing.

"Pretty badass, huh?" I declared proudly as the forest glowed with warm light.

"Much better than a torch," Boone agreed.

I turned to the hawthorn and said a silent prayer. I didn't know what was going to happen tonight, but I asked for something good. If the universe couldn't give me that, then something half decent. Boone needed something to hold onto. Eventually, there would be a chapter in our story when I wasn't going to be enough. Not with this.

"It's not a coincidence," he said as I placed my hands on the tree. "The wolves were chasin' me the first night. A wolf was stalkin' you when you first arrived. Then I changed into one meself. I might know somethin' that could help you fight Carman. At least, understandin' what I did to break through that barrier…that could help. The risk is worth it."

"It's a can of worms," I said with a frown when the Crescents didn't answer.

It didn't mean anything. Sometimes, they weren't there at all and only came through when the moon was at its brightest, though I suspected they only spoke up when they had something to say. Not a bunch for small talk, then.

"Aye, I know I'm takin' a risk." He shrugged and raked his fingers through his hair. "I don't know what else to do. I'm limited in me powers. What can I do to help you against another witch? Nothin'."

My shoulders sagged, and I grasped his hand. Boone had reached breaking point.

"You've done a lot already," I murmured. "More than you realize."

He grasped my shoulders, his eyes shining in the semidarkness. "If I knew how I changed into that wolf, then maybe I can do more."

"Boone…" I didn't like where this was going.

"I want to try to change," he said, voicing my fears. "Will you help me?"

"But you… Boone, you were almost feral."

"It was me emotions," he argued. "You were dyin', and I was desperate."

"I don't know." I shied away, knowing he was probably going to try changing anyway. If I were here or not, it didn't make a difference.

"I have to figure it out, Skye. It may be the key to unlockin' me memories."

"So that's what this is about?"

He let me go, his brow furrowing.

"Then change and find out," I said. "I'd rather be here while you did, than not."

He nodded and began stripping. I folded his clothes into a neat pile as he shed each piece, setting them on a squishy patch of moss so they would stay clean. Glancing up, I got the perfect view of tonight's full moon.

"Strange, I thought it was a waxing crescent tonight," I quipped.

"Stop lookin' at me ass like that," he complained.

"I can't help it. It's a good ass."

"Good?" He glanced over his shoulder.

"Amazeballs?" I offered.

"Now you're just gettin' filthy."

"You knew what I was like before you got involved." I smiled, thankful for the mood lifter. "I'm here. Do what you've gotta do."

His shoulders tensed, and he knelt in the center of the clearing. I took a step back, giving him the space he needed to attempt his change. The muscles in his back rippled, and I winced as his bones began to snap, and his flesh began to distort.

I never liked watching Boone change. If I were being honest, I tried not to witness it at all. The pain came with the ability, and he'd developed a tolerance for it. He'd assured me—which was often—but tonight…something wasn't right.

Boone grunted, holding onto a cry as his arms and legs grew. His knees snapped backward, and he lowered his head, trying to hide his change from me best he could. His snout was growing, his skin was sprouting fur, and the beginning of a tail was appearing, but his change was slow and cumbersome.

He was struggling and attempting to force the shape to come forth.

"Boone, stop!" I exclaimed, wanting to touch him. It was the worst thing I could do while he was like this. A single touch could send him into a frenzy.

He put his head down and gritted his teeth, his bones continuing to snap. Either he couldn't stop…or he *didn't want to*.

"*Stop!*" I cried again. "This is stupid! You're hurting yourself!"

Boone snarled as his face elongated, and his teeth grew, then he turned on me, his jaws snapping. I stumbled back a step, my heart racing. The beast was rising to the surface. It had frightened me the night of the ritual, but now it was beginning to terrify me.

He was half man, half something else, struggling with his change. He'd always been so fluid when he'd morphed into his familiars. The fox and the gyrfalcon. Even when he'd told me about how he'd made an affinity with Mark Ashlyn's stallion, it had seemed easy for him, so why was the wolf shape so difficult? Maybe it was the block in his mind, and the only thing that had broken through that night was his link with me.

"Boone!" I cried. "Stop! You'll get stuck! You'll get stuck and won't be able to come back!"

His jaws snapped at me, but I pushed past the fear and threw myself at him. I collided against his chest, and his arms wrapped around me, and his claws dug into my back.

My magic pulsed through me and into him. The impact sent a soundless shockwave out through the clearing and into the forest, the force rattling the trees and dislodging leaves from their ancient boughs. I didn't know what else to do, what words to chant or intent to put behind it. I just asked him to come back.

He disappeared from my grasp, and I fell forward onto the ground, jarring my wrists. A muffled yelp echoed from beneath me, and my eyes widened as I saw the familiar shape of a fox pinned under my startled body. He wasn't the russet color I was used to seeing—with his white chest and belly and black-tipped ears—but a sparkling silver and gray. His feet were black, and so were his nose and ears, but the rest of him… It was like someone had taken all the color from his coat.

Boone rose to his paws and shook, his silver tail flicking back and forth as he wriggled out from underneath me. He glanced at me, his black eyes full of questions I didn't have any answers to.

"I'd make a joke about being a silver fox, but…" I shrugged and stroked his fur. "Don't stay like that too long."

He blinked, then padded away from me. His change back to human seemed to go easier on his body, and before long, he was a butt-naked Irishman once more.

"You scared me half to death!" I exclaimed, throwing my arms around his neck.

"Careful," he said, wincing at my touch.

Pulling back, I poked and prodded at his limbs until he pulled away and sat his bare ass in the dirt.

"I can feel it in there," he said, fisting his hands into his wild hair. "But it's locked away like me memories. I can't get to it."

"You don't have an affinity with it," I said. When he glared at me, I added, "Maybe you did before, but you've forgotten it. Something allowed you to tap into it the other night, but now it's gone again. We've gotta figure out what that something was."

Boone glanced away and shivered. The cold was starting get to him, and the heat his shapeshifter body usually radiated wasn't helping the closer winter came.

"Somethin' is changin'," he murmured. "I can feel it."

I picked up his shirt and draped it over his shoulders. His fox shape had been silver this time. I wondered if it was going to be a permanent thing and if tonight had triggered a change in his abilities he couldn't stop.

"The wolf is leechin' into me other forms... I was afraid it might happen."

"So?" I asked, rubbing his shoulders. "A healing tongue and the ability to negate magical barriers sounds like a useful ability, right?"

Boone nodded but didn't look comforted. He was too wrapped up in the why. Hopefully, that part would come, but I knew it wouldn't all at once. Sometimes, things had to reveal themselves over time and forcing the issue caused more harm than good. Tonight was a prime example of that. He could've become stuck between shapes, and then where would we be?

"I know you want answers, Boone, and I want them for you too, but..." I sighed and kissed his cheek. "I don't want you to hurt yourself finding them. Not like this. It's selfish as hell, but I need you."

"And I need you, Skye, but... But..." He was struggling. The failure to change into the elusive wolf troubled him more than I would ever understand.

"You have to be satisfied for now," I murmured. "Patience... You can't force it."

He nodded, trying to hide the pain from his expression. His attempt had hurt him more than he was admitting.

"Let's go home, okay?" I reached for his clothes. "How about a hot bath? Doesn't that sound good? You're freezing."

"Skye." His big hand cupped my cheek, silencing me mid-babble.

I sighed and rested my forehead against his.

"We'll figure it out," he said. "We always do."

I hoped he was right.

CHAPTER 5

The weeks began to pass, and nothing changed in Derrydun. Nothing out of the unordinary, anyway.

Mary Donnelly was still planning a spring wedding for Boone and me, Sean McKinnon was still drunk and pining after his dead wife, Mrs. Boyle had upgraded her broom to a shovel to see her through winter, and the tourist buses had stopped altogether. Apart from an odd group of backpackers or a lone rental car day-tripping from the big cities, the quiet village life had simmered down to a faint blip on the ol' heart monitor. It seemed hibernation was a thing when the sky threatened ice and snow.

As he'd predicted, Boone's various animal shapes had all turned silver, though he didn't have any trouble shifting like he had the night he'd attempted to recreate his mysterious wolf form. His gyrfalcon shape had always bordered on silver and white anyway, so it felt comforting to him that something was the same. Unlike me.

Ever since I'd paid a visit to the Nightshade Witches, I'd been struggling with the terrible burden of being a Crescent Witch. I understood their hatred now. Being a leader sometimes meant you had to do bad things for the greater good, and the legacy I was a part of had done things I wasn't proud of. Now I'd added my own chapter to the darker side of the story. Taking the birthright of an entire coven was an awful punishment. I could justify it however I wanted, but it still burned a hole inside me.

And there'd been no blips on the radar from Carman or any other malicious fae or craglorn. It was mysteriously quiet.

I worked on my magic, Boone experimented with his newly acquired magical tongue, and Mairead built up the colors on her Derrydun landscape painting that she'd moved from the garden shed into the laundry at the back of the cottage.

We prepared, we watched, and we waited.

Then, one morning in late October, the world started to change.

Rolling out of bed, something felt different. It was cold —there was nothing new or strange about that—but the air felt close. Shaking it off, I showered and dressed, making sure I put on my thermal undies I'd bought off the Internet the week before. I was so not used to having numb ass cheeks.

Thundering down that stars, I checked the laundry in case Mairead was locked in there high on paint fumes, but the room was empty. I looked over her work in progress and let out a *humph*.

The canvas was still one big blob of color, but she'd already begun the fine detailing. It was actually starting to look like something now. There was the powerhouse with the tangle of ivy clinging to its facade and the spire of the church through the forest.

"Not bad, kid," I muttered.

Galloping into the kitchen, I snatched out a breakfast bar, unwrapped it, and shoved the end in my mouth. Glancing at the clock as I pulled on my gloves and beanie, I groaned. Mairead would already be at Irish Moon waiting for me. Today was day one of stocktaking, and I was so not looking forward to it. Count all the things, take photos of said things, and start building the most epic website in the history of epic websites. I knew how to turn on a computer, but that was about it. The rest was going to be a comedy of errors and curse words.

Opening the door, I breathed out a plume of vaporized air around the breakfast bar still shoved in my mouth. It took me a full minute to realize that overnight it had snowed. In October? Weird.

I scratched my head, knowing Boone had been pulling my leg when he'd told me it snowed in Derrydun. The gig was up the moment I'd typed 'does it snow in Ireland' into Google. This was abnormal.

It was so still and close. Nothing stirred among the whiteness, and for a second, I felt like the only person left in the world.

The garden was lost under a few inches of white stuff. Cold snap, indeed. I totally got the powder reference until I plunged my bare hand into the drift by the side of the cottage. The cold burned my skin, and I pulled back, wiping the water on my jeans. It wasn't grandma-scented talcum powder at all! My winter wonderland fantasy exploded into a billion tiny icicles, and I stepped down onto the path.

My boot slipped on the ice, and I threw my arms out to steady myself. *Close call.*

Making my way cautiously down the path, I decided even though it was beautiful, snow was treacherously deceptive. There was a metaphor in there someplace, but my brain was too frozen to dwell on it.

Out of nowhere, a ball of mushed-together snow smacked into the side of my head. I let out an *oomph* and slipped on the ice. Landing on my ass, I yelped as both cheeks began to throb, and my breakfast bar plopped into the snow.

"*Bull's-eye!*" Mairead exclaimed, jumping out from her hiding spot.

"*Mairead!*" I shrieked. "I was having a magical moment, and you ruined it! And I can't find my breakfast!"

"Sore loser," she declared with a pout.

Bunching up a wad of ice in my hands, I scowled. "I thought snow was meant to be powder soft like cute little cotton balls."

"That's clouds."

"I thought it didn't snow around here," I complained, my thermal undies well and truly feeling like I'd peed my pants…without the warmth.

"Sometimes," she replied. "It's been really cold this year."

I wondered why that was. I rolled my eyes and shoved the unwelcome thoughts of magical mischief into the back of my mind. My supernatural spidey sense wasn't tingling in the slightest. *It could just be really cold because it's just really cold*, I thought to myself with an added twist of sarcasm for my own benefit.

I packed together the ice in my hand and smiled as my thoughts turned wicked. Throwing the snowball at Mairead, it smacked her right in the guts, and she doubled over with an *oomph*. Doing a commando-style roll, I leaped to my feet, slipped, and dove behind the fence.

"That hurt!" she screeched.

"Who's a sore loser now?" I called out from behind my hiding spot. "You can dish it out, but can't take it, I see!"

"This is war!"

"Bring it on!"

Thud! Snow showered over the top of the fence, dusting me with a layer of ice.

Popping my head over the top, I threw another missile at Mairead, who didn't have any cover she could dart behind. The snowball flew straight past her and smacked into a tree.

"You suck," the Goth girl taunted.

I ducked back behind the fence and started balling up snow, making a neat line of ammo. Choosing the largest, I peered over the edge and surveyed the battlefield.

"What's goin' on here?"

At the sound of Boone's voice, Mairead and I turned at the same time and smiled wickedly at each other. Hurling our collective arsenal, Boone let out a surprised *oomph* as snowball after snowball collided with him. His arms flailed, and his boots slid back and forth as he tried to keep his balance.

"*I surrender!*" he cried, then promptly slipped and fell on his ass.

We burst out into fits of laughter, and I skidded my way out from behind the fence. Holding my hand out for Boone, he grasped it and yanked me down. We fell in a heap as Mairead held her side, obviously finding our predicament the funniest thing she'd ever seen.

I squealed as snow found its way down my top, and I managed to find my feet again. Boone sprang up beside me like a professional, and I pouted. Shaking myself off, little clumps of ice flew everywhere.

"You're both on the hit list," I declared. "I've got wet knickers."

"*Eww*," Mairead shouted. "That's me cue to leave." She feigned throwing up and darted across the lawn, skidded across the path, smacked into the side of the shop, then disappeared around the corner.

"She's too easy," I said with a laugh.

"You're as bad as each other," Boone said, swatting at his jumper and knocking off clumps of snow. He had on a thick, grayish woolly sweater with an elaborate, and slightly dorky, cable-knit pattern. He looked different without his trademark red and black checkered shirt.

"Well, that was a way to wake up." I pressed the backs of my gloves against my flushed cheeks. "I've cracked a sweat."

"Are you sure it's sweat?"

"Stop it." I swatted at his arm.

"Ack," he grumbled. "I thought you'd be stayin' in today."

"We're starting stocktake today," I replied, helping him brush himself off. "What kind of jumper is this anyway? Cable knit? Wasn't that big in the eighties?"

"'Tis Aran wool," he stated, puffing out his chest. "And it's a sweater."

"Is that meant to be special?"

"To be sure. It's wool from the Aran Islands off the west coast of Ireland. 'Tis famous."

"If you say so. You look like a fisherman."

"They're known as Fisherman Sweaters, too."

"You're not selling me on it."

"So, I just came to see how you like the snow," he declared, changing the subject.

"Nice save."

He grinned and pulled down my beanie.

"Hey!" I yanked it off and smacked him in the chest with it. "I'm dealing with the snow just fine. For all of the five minutes I've been outside in it."

"Aye, we got quite a bit of it."

I frowned, glancing over the yard. "More than usual?"

"We get maybe two or three falls each winter," he explained. "This is more than I've ever seen, and earlier, but I have limited memories to pull from." He knew so much about everything that it was easy to forget his collective life memories were barely four years old. "I suppose it could happen naturally."

I didn't want to say what was on my mind, but I didn't have to. Boone looked troubled, too. He had that forehead crease thing going on.

"The weather is weird all over," he went on. "It doesn't mean anythin'. El Niño?"

"La Niña," I replied, hoping it was some freakish weather thing and not a smoke screen for Carman's advancement toward the ancient hawthorn.

"What's the difference?"

"El Niño is dry. La Niña is wet."

Boone smirked.

"Don't be dirty." Suddenly, my mood had dampened along with my knickers.

"I'm goin' to help out Roy today," he went on. "It's too slippery on the roads to be drivin' for Mary."

"Give me a kiss before you go, then."

He slid his hands around my waist, pulled me close, and planted one right on my lips. As an added bonus, he tilted his head to the side and gave me a little tongue to go with it.

"What a treat," I murmured. "Now my undies are sopping."

"Don't yell at Mairead too much today."

"So not the time to talk about Mairead." I rolled my eyes and rested my forehead against his.

"I'll cook you dinner tonight."

"You say all the right things."

He grinned and let me go. Walking across the lawn, his boots squeaked on the snow.

Glancing up at the sky, I didn't like the color. It was gray and heavy, and nothing broke it up. Not even swirls or loose puffs of cotton wool. It was like one giant cloud was sitting over the entire country like a creepy blanket come to suffocate us all.

"Boone?" I called out, a wave of nausea rolling through my stomach.

He turned, and I decided his fancy Aran sweater wasn't so dorky after all. As if he could read the uneasiness in my mind, he smiled.

"We're too few to be proactive," he said, his voice slightly muffled by all the ice. "We're doin' all we can."

I nodded. No matter how many times he kept telling me, there was a part of me that still needed to hear it. I watched him move off through the winter wonderland, his breath puffing up in plumes as he went. Once he was gone, I began to feel rather alone.

Brushing off my jeans, I slipped and slid around to Irish Moon, the hairs on the back of my neck prickling. Not from the cold but my brewing paranoia. Opening the door, I stepped into the blissful warmth of the shop. Mairead was behind the counter, scrolling on her mobile phone.

"While you were playing tonsil hockey, Maggie

dropped this off." She waved a bit of paper in the air, not even glancing up from Snapchat or Candy Crush Saga or whatever app was the rage with the kids these days.

"What's this for?" Reaching over the counter, I snatched it out of her hand and read the front. It was a party invitation.

"Samhain," she replied. "Molly McCreedy's."

"Sowin?" I made a face.

"S-A-M-H-A-I-N," she spelled out. "*Halloween*." She punctuated the end of the sentence with a dramatic roll of her eyes.

"Oh, *Sam-hain*."

Mairead snorted and rolled her eyes.

"Don't make fun of my innocent lack of Wiccan holiday knowledge. I don't think I've ever said that word out loud before let alone heard someone say it. I didn't exactly know any other witches before I was so unceremoniously tricked into moving to Ireland."

"Is that what you call it? I thought you were just complainin'."

I shot Mairead a bitchy look and read over the invite again. Costumes mandatory. *Ugh*. I always hated dressing up. I was the kind of person who would turn up in her usual clothes, and when people asked who I was, I would make a smartass comment that I'd come 'as myself.'

Though this year was a different story. I was an actual witch with actual magical powers and a shapeshifter boyfriend. I wouldn't be surprised if ghosts and that headless horseman fellow were a thing.

I slumped my shoulders and sighed. "I wonder if there's anything to it."

"To what?"

"The ghosts and shit."

"Ghosts and shit?" Her cheeks paled, which was a feat considering her skin tone was translucent at best.

"Costumes are mandatory?" I shook the bit of paper, completely outraged. "Who makes costumes mandatory?"

"Maggie," Mairead stated.

"What am I supposed to go as?"

"I always go as myself," the Goth girl said. "Every day is Halloween to me."

I almost choked on my own spit and fell to the floor.

"I should go as a sexy witch, then," I retorted. "And Boone can get a fox costume, and we'd all be ironic a-holes."

"If we're all going as ourselves, then you need to take out the sexy part."

"*Mairead!*" I pouted and put my hands on my hips.

A party, huh? Maybe it was just the thing we needed to lift our spirits. I smirked, thinking about getting that sexy witch costume. Mostly to annoy Mairead, but Boone would be really into it...*in a wet knicker kind of way.*

"Give me the computer! *Stat!*" I declared. "I've got some online shopping to do!"

CHAPTER 6

I hated the nights Boone worked at Molly McCreedy's.

Looking at my empty microwave meal tray, I sighed. I'd gotten used to his home cooking, and nuked chicken wasn't the same. Mairead was smart. She'd shaken her head at the prospect of rubberized beef and disappeared into the laundry with her painting.

Glancing at the overflowing bin, I angled my head to the side. If I anchored the corner of the container on that wad of aluminum foil and propped the other end against that empty popcorn bag, then I wouldn't have to go outside in the dark, and trash mountain would still be standing tall.

Holding my breath, I gingerly put the container into place…and the whole thing crashed to the floor, making a huge mess. Grumbling, I cleaned up and tied a knot in the top of the bag. Seriously, what was the point of being a witch if I couldn't do cool things like make a mop wipe the floor on its own or make the trash take itself out? I laughed to myself at the thought. Now, there was an idea. I could spell Carman to take herself out. That would solve all our problems.

If only it were that easy.

Lifting up the trash, I opened the back door and gasped, dropping the garbage bag onto the floor.

A silver wolf emerged from the darkness, all big and wild, and all I could see were teeth. It lopped up the garden path, its big paws thumping on the ground like an elephant was galloping toward the cottage. Calling on my magic, I stretched out my hands.

"Stay back!" I cried. "Or I'll... I'll..." I didn't know what I was going to do but blasting its ass across the garden sounded like a fantastic idea. I'd poked out a shapeshifter wolf's eye once before, and if he'd come back for seconds, I would make the other one pop.

The wolf skidded to a halt, like it had the ultimate clumsy gene, and sat on its haunches. It tilted its head to the side and watched me with interest. Finally, it let out a whimper and licked its lips. Two big eyes stared at me, and I curled my outstretched fingers into a fist, dampening my magic.

"*Boone?*"

The wolf's tail thumped on the stoop.

"You're kidding me!" I threw my hands up into the air, letting the last of my magic dissipate. "I was going to make your head explode!"

Wolf-Boone weaved past me into the kitchen, practically trampling me he was so big. I closed the door as he began to change into his human form, the sound of snapping and popping bones making me wince. It sounded worse than usual and was no easier to hear.

Turning on my heel, I glared at his hot, Irish, naked body. How could I be mad at him when he looked like a

Calvin Klein model… *Wait.* I was so not going to be swayed by a six-pack and a tight ass. I was so mad at him for scaring me half to death!

"I think you could do it now," he said.

"Do what?" I exclaimed. "Use my magical palms as a defibrillator on my own chest?"

"Unlock me memories."

"*Pfft.*" I crossed my arms and deepened my glare. If I stared hard enough, I might be able to shoot magical lasers out of my eyes. Now, that would be something. "You're lucky Mairead has noise-canceling headphones. She's listening to Marilyn Manson, Nine Inch Nails, or whatever the Goth kids like these days out in the laundry. Imagine what she would've done in her pants if she'd come out here and found a giant wolf sitting on the back step." Snatching up a tea towel, I thrust it at him. "And cover your dingleberries."

"Will you help?" he asked, covering up his junk with the floral-printed tea towel.

"I thought you were that other wolf," I said with a pout. "The one-eyed thing. The creepy dude you said was another shapeshifter."

"Sorry," he said sheepishly.

"You went out and changed into a bloody wolf without me," I exclaimed, slapping him on the arm. My palm cracked against his skin, and he yelped. "You could've got stuck!"

"It was an accident," he complained, rubbing his bicep.

"You have to deliberately will yourself to change, so I don't see how that could happen."

"I was changin' into me fox form," he explained. "I guess it's been on me mind a lot, the whole wolf thing, and it just… It overtook me. Before I knew what was happenin'…"

I eyed him warily. "You had control over it this time."

Boone nodded. "I wasn't lost in the animal like I was then. It felt like…" He drew in a deep breath. "It felt like me other shapes. Familiar."

I worried my bottom lip, the garbage bag forgotten beside the door. Maybe the wolf form was his original familiar, unlike the fox shape he took after he'd lost his memory. He'd said it was the first form he remembered taking, so it stood to reason it would be his first go to.

"I think who I was is starting to leech into who I am now," he said. "Whatever happened the night I first changed, it must've triggered somethin'. A leak or a crack… Somethin's different, Skye. I think you could get through."

The silver… I sighed, knowing he could be right. Something *was* leeching into his shapeshifter forms, changing them to the point his coat had changed colors. The russet fox was silver, and his gyrfalcon was pure white with a silver belly. I was entirely sure his black stallion would be silver, too, though he never used that shape.

"Have you been getting headaches?" I asked.

He shook his head. "They're not as bad."

Was the spell eroding? Something strange was going on, and we couldn't explain it. His memories might be forcing their way out, but there was only one way to—

A blood-curdling scream tore through the kitchen, and I turned to find Mairead standing in the doorway, her gaze fixed on the tea towel over Boone's junk.

"We're going out," I said, standing in front of the naked Irishman. "Don't wait up."

"Why is he naked? What's going on?"

"There are several words for this," I said to Boone, "and they all result in being arrested."

"Or having me ass whipped with a lamp cord," he said wryly.

"Kinky," I murmured.

Boone began backing away slowly, waving at Mairead with his free hand. "See you later."

"You better wash that tea towel before you bring it back!" the Goth girl shouted after us.

Closing the door behind us, I smirked at Boone. "Don't forget the fabric softener. My dishes prefer to be caressed with soft, sweet-smelling material."

After a quick stop off to collect Boone's clothes from the bush he'd hidden them under, we made our way down the path toward the ancient hawthorn. By the time we reached the clearing, I'd managed to calm down. Boone had terrible timing, but I doubted he'd tried to scare me. Who knew I would shake off the laziness and actually take out the rubbish? No one could predict miracles.

"Are you sure you want to do this?" I asked, the familiar closeness of the tree surrounding me like a fluffy blanket. Too bad it wasn't a warm blanket. I was freezing my *you-know-whats* off.

"There's never goin' to be a good time," Boone replied.

"Right." I cracked my knuckles and shook out my arms. "Let's split this thing wide open."

"Be careful," Boone said, his brow creasing. "Last time didn't end very well."

"I'll try not to blow myself across the clearing. Don't worry."

"Skye, do you know what you're doin'?'"

"Not really," I replied, unfazed. "My magic is instinctual, which means I'll know it when I see it."

"Which really means you're stabbin' in the dark."

"Am not!" I hesitated, then sighed, my shoulders sagging. "Okay. I am, but curing amnesia wasn't in the handbook. Give me a break."

Ignoring Boone's concerned look, I took a deep breath. How was I supposed to do this? Reaching out, I put both my hands on his head.

"Is this part of it?" he asked.

"Shh!"

I rolled my shoulders back a few times and entered my mind. Imagining my fingers digging into Boone's brain, I felt my magic work its way from my body into his. At first, it felt strange, like a million pins and needles in my fingertips, but then I could feel him. It was a strange almost out-of-body sensation. I moved from myself into him. Not in the psychical sense. It was a spiritual thing.

Sensing a hard shell over parts of his being—the bits and pieces someone desperately wanted him to forget—I assumed this was what Aileen had seen when she'd tried to break the amnesia spell. At least, a version of it.

A metallic silver glow was pulsating from the middle of the shell, the glow reaching an intensity it was almost too hard to look at. This must be the fissure Boone had sensed, and the one that had allowed him to shift into the wolf in the first place. There was a very silver theme going on, but it was a glaring indicator that this was the place to break into. Go for the weak spot, and the entire spell would crumble. At least, that was how the theory went.

Focusing, I nudged a thread of golden light into the silver, coaxing it to work its way through the shell. If this was Boone's essence, then it was trying to break free, right? Why else would there be a crack in the spell? No one could contain someone's true nature for long, especially if it were as wild as Boone's nature.

C'mon, I thought. *Come out, and show me who you are. Remember what they took from you. You want to come out, don't you?*

The silver light flared, and before I could do anything about it, my connection with Boone was severed, and I was flying backward through the air like a human cannonball.

My head cracked against a fallen tree, and all the air left my lungs. I wheezed, trying to catch my breath. Rolling onto my side, I felt like throwing up as blood whooshed in my ears.

"Skye!" Boone was beside me in a flash, his hands helping me into an upright position.

"Wow," I rasped, then erupted in a fit of coughing.

He rubbed my back and started picking dried leaves out of my hair. "Are you all right?"

Glancing across the clearing, I snorted. "I must've flown at least fifteen meters." Wincing, I rubbed the back of my head. When I pulled my hand away, I expected to find blood smeared across it, but thankfully, there was nothing there.

"You hit your head pretty hard," Boone said. He placed his hand on my face and tilted me toward him. Checking my eyes, he frowned.

"Am I in trouble, doc?" I asked with a dose of sarcasm.

"*Skye.*"

I knew he was dying to ask me what I'd seen, but I couldn't tell him anything. Just the light and the explosion, like whoever or whatever was lurking behind there wanted to push me away.

Did Boone *want* to forget?

On the surface, he might say he wanted to remember, but deep down, was he afraid of something? Whatever it was, I didn't want to acknowledge it, either.

"There was…" I hesitated, and the hopeful look in his eyes broke my heart.

"I don't remember anythin'," he said, saving me the pain of telling him what he already knew.

"I can see the crack…but there's no way in. I… I'm sorry, Boone."

He rose, the frustration clear on his face.

"It's okay," he said. "Maybe some stones are best left unturned."

I pushed ungracefully to my feet and grasped his arm to steady myself. There were no more words of encouragement in me. He'd heard them all before and saying them now… Well, it felt like rubbing salt into an open wound.

"I better see you home," he finally said.

I wasn't going to argue.

The entire walk home, my head spun.

"You don't look so good," Boone said, weaving his arm through mine.

I rubbed my forehead. "I bumped my head."

"I'm sorry. I dragged you out here again, and it still didn't work."

"It's fine," I said, shaking my head. "It's just about the only thing we can be proactive about. I had to try. Besides, it's good practice."

"I don't know about that."

"You said your headaches are getting better. That's a good thing, I suppose."

Boone grunted, signaling he wasn't keen on talking about it anymore. It must hurt. All the trying and failing.

By the time we reached the cottage, I was feeling a lot better even though the world felt...fuzzy. I was sure something was definitely hanging around, and it wasn't a concussion. Something felt different, but for the life of me, I couldn't figure it out.

That night, my sleep was full of dreams.

There was a swirl of images, feelings, and emotions that were so intense, I felt like I was being dragged under a raging torrent. It reminded me of the sluagh at the spring underneath Croagh Patrick, their inky fingers tearing at my clothes, pulling me into a watery grave, their hunger for my magic absolute.

It felt like summer. My feet were bare, dirt and leaves creeping between my toes. Overhead, I felt the protective blanket of the hawthorn's power, and I turned toward the great tree. What was I doing out here with no shoes on? My feet were totally delicate. There was a reason I wore big, kick-ass boots, and it wasn't all about being able to kick craglorns in *their* delicate parts with the steel caps.

My gaze was drawn to the tree, the soles of my feet forgotten in an instant.

A door was set into the base of the hawthorn, but it didn't look like anything I'd imagined. When I thought of the way to the fae realm, I had a vision of a swirling portal of magic like the wormhole on that science fiction show *Stargate*. A rippling puddle of energy you had to step through to make it to the other side.

This doorway was bland and ordinary. Honestly, it looked like the round door to a hobbit hole. I shouldn't be so surprised that I got the fantasy references Ireland was famous for. That was why they filmed all those big-budget television phenomenons here.

I was so not falling for this. This was a test, right? Don't open the door that all the bad things are supposed to come out of like Pandora's box. Curiosity killed the Crescent Witch and all of that.

Don't open the door. *Open the door, Skye.*

Reaching out, I grasped the wrought iron handle and twisted. The latch unhooked, and I pulled...

I sat bolt upright, my chest heaving and my thoughts all fuzzy.

"Purple alligator monkey typewriter thing-a-ma-whatsit!" I exclaimed, causing Boone to jerk awake.

"Skye?" He pushed up and rubbed his hand over my back. "What's wrong?"

I rubbed my eyes, clearing the last of my dream from my mind's eye. There was something about a... *Wait.* Dammit! The images were already starting to fade. I had a feeling it had been something important. Something I needed to... Needed to what? Do, say, go? Was it something I needed to stop Carman?

"I had a dream. There was something about a purple typewriter," I said. "And an alligator and a...monkey?"

"Skye, you're not makin' any sense." He frowned, but I wasn't paying much attention.

I stuck my tongue out and wiped it with my palms. "Purple monkey. Typewriter."

Boone grasped my face in his hands and pulled me toward him. His eyes sparkled in the murky light, his concern palpable.

"Alligator?" I asked, my eyebrows knitting together.

"Ack, maybe you did hit your head too hard."

"No, it's the..." It was the dream. "The door..."

Flopping back on the bed, I stared at the ceiling. I was beginning to understand how Boone felt. Whatever I'd seen in my dream was gone and had only left a pile of purple alligator typewriter monkey nonsense in its place. Anyway, what was the purple thing? The alligator or the monkey? Or were they all purple? The orientation kept changing like an annoying Rubick's Cube. One side was all the one color, but the others…

"I'm fine," I muttered, turning onto my side. "Go back to sleep."

"Skye…" His hand slid around my waist.

"I just need some sleep. I'm overtired. I'll be okay in the morning. Promise."

He grunted and tightened his grip on me. We lay like that for ages before Boone drifted off to sleep again. His breathing evened out, and my eyes remained wide open, dwelling on the purple alligator and the monkey typewriter.

Finally, as the night began to fade into dawn outside, I fell back asleep, unable to shake the feeling that I'd opened something that should've remained closed.

CHAPTER 7

Glancing around the kitchen, I studied every nook and cranny in an attempt to figure out why I felt so…out of place.

"What are you doin'?" Boone asked, looking up from his Weetabix.

"I'm trying to find the glitch in the Matrix," I said, squinting at the tablecloth.

"Huh?" He made a face.

"We need to get Netflix," I said, scratching at the fabric. "Your pop culture knowledge is severely lacking."

"Are you sure you didn't break somethin' last night?" he asked putting his spoon down. "You had a rough landin'."

"I don't know," I murmured, lost in my own thoughts. "I'm sure it's just the bump on the head."

Boone went back to his Weetabix, but I couldn't shake the feeling that something in his mind didn't want me in there. The more I dwelled on it, the more I knew that I hadn't hit an invisible electric fence but something—or someone—had shoved me out. I wondered if Aileen had felt the same thing. The bump on the head hadn't helped, either.

Whatever it was, something dark had locked away Boone's memories, and I couldn't help wondering if it, and the wolves that had been chasing him the night he'd come to Derrydun, had something to do with Carman.

I guessed time would tell…about all of it.

Still sensing I was off-kilter, Boone wouldn't let up get me. He fussed and clucked like a mother hen until I was forced to send him to the convenience store at the Topaz up the street to get some peace and quiet. Coffee tasted like dirty dishwater on my taste buds, and after last night's awful sleep, I needed a carton of energy drink.

Thankfully, Mairead was super independent and didn't need to wait for us to pour herself a bowl of Rice Bubbles before disappearing off to wherever Goth girls went before nine a.m. around here.

Boone wasn't back before it was time to leave for Irish Moon. Assuming he'd been accosted by a random villager for a lengthy chat, I dragged my sorry behind into the crystal mecca without my hit of sugar-laced taurine.

"You look like you've been punched in the eye," Mairead said as I did a zombie lurch across the shop floor.

I poked my tongue out at her and rounded the counter. Pulling out the tarot cards, I held them in my hands and shuffled, hoping the energy of the familiar and the resonance of the crystals could soothe the uneasiness I'd felt since waking up spouting nonsense.

It all started when the block on Boone's mind threw me across the clearing, I thought to myself. *He zapped me unknowingly, and now I'm all weird.* I was really worried he'd short-circuited my magical solenoids.

"We've still got a million pictures to take for the

website," Mairead complained when I sat down like a lump and didn't move.

"I just want to draw a card," I said. "I've been neglecting them lately."

She leaned against the counter, watching me shuffle. "Okay, let's see, then."

Selecting a card, I pulled it out of the deck. Seeing my old friend the Chariot, I curled my lip.

"*Pfft*." I flung the card down on the counter. "Upside down Chariot. *Again*. So not helpful."

"Go again?" the Goth girl offered.

I sighed and slipped the card back into the deck. Humoring her, I shuffled and pulled another card. Flipping it over, it revealed the Chariot reversed.

"See? It's no use," I said, putting the card back into the deck for the second time. "This has happened before. No matter how many times I shuffle, split the deck, fling them all up into the air…" I sighed dramatically and spread the cards across the counter in a long fanned out line. "Watch this."

I tapped a card and flicked it out of the lineup. Turning it over, the familiar golden lines of the Chariot showed her face.

"Chariot, Chariot, Chariot!" I exclaimed. "All upside down. All the time."

"Why?" Mairead asked, looking mystified. "It's a little creepy, but there's gotta be a reason, right?"

"Yeah, whatever this card heralds, there's no escaping it." I made a face and tidied up the tarot cards, then dropped them back into their box. "Totally comforting when I feel like I've got the hangover to end all hangovers."

"You're hung over?" It was Mairead's turn to pull an unattractive expression.

"Don't do that," I said, getting out the little digital camera from under the counter. "You look like a slapped ass."

"You're so mean. Gimme that."

She grabbed the camera, and the moment our fingers touched, a bolt of static electricity crackled.

"*Ow!*" Mairead exclaimed, almost dropping the camera.

"Purple typewriter monkey!" I exclaimed.

"Purple what?" Her look went from shocked to *time to call the asylum and have Skye locked up* in two seconds flat.

Testing a theory, I reached out and poked the back of her hand. Another zap crackled, and she leaped away from me.

"Ow! What are you doin'?"

"I feel weird," I replied, shaking my tingling hand. *I was supercharged or something…*

"You feel weird? You better not be doin' that on purpose."

"The last time I was this full of static was when…" I trailed off. The last time I was zapping everything was after Aileen had died, and the Crescent Calling was trying to drag me to Derrydun.

Something magical was going on here. I wanted to say *duh*, like how couldn't I realize it, but something was in my head, screwing with my thought patterns. Was it the same thing or something different? Who the hell knew.

The door opened, and the bell jingled merrily.

"I've got a delivery for Skye Williams?"

"Oh! Oh! That's me!" I jumped up at the sight of the mailman and made grabby hand gestures for the parcel in his hands.

Our hands brushed, and immediately, the air zinged with static as the mother of all shocks went up his arm.

"Hell!" he cursed, shaking his hand.

Mairead's mouth dropped open, and I felt my cheeks heat.

"How weird," I said, scratching my head.

"Yeah…" The mailman grimaced and backed away toward the door.

Frowning, I turned away, slightly embarrassed I'd zapped a complete stranger. Hugging the parcel to my chest, I sighed. How inconvenient.

"Are you sure you're not doing that on purpose?" Mairead asked when he'd left.

"Of course, I'm sure!" I exclaimed. "I don't get my jollies going around shocking random strangers."

"You're gettin' weirder by the day." She nodded at the parcel. "What's that, then?"

"It's my Halloween costume!" I declared, tearing open the plastic with a flourish.

Holding up the packet, I grinned.

"A sexy witch?" Mairead raised her eyebrows. "Case in point."

"I told you I wasn't messing around." I grinned, my static charge forgotten for the time being. "Best costume *ever.*"

***

"I thought costumes were compulsory!"

Boone stood on the front step, wearing his usual getup of jeans, boots, black and red checkered shirt, tight black T-shirt, and his ratty leather bomber jacket. While I appreciated his penchant for tight underthings, I was so not unimpressed.

To think I'd gone to all the trouble of ordering a costume online when I loathed dressing up. The fishnet stockings I'd loaned off Mairead began to itch my crotch area, and I wondered how anyone wore these things. Picking an itchy front wedgie was so not sexy. Even more so when your costume was a sexy witch…*not itch*.

He shrugged and buried his hands deeper into his pockets.

"*Typical.*" I pouted.

"Are you goin' to show me what's under that coat?"

"Nope." I smiled sweetly, tightened the trench coat I'd found in Aileen's closet, and shook my head. "Not until we get to Molly McCreedy's."

"It better be appropriate for all ages."

I rolled my eyes, knowing the fishnet stockings were only appropriate on two occasions. When you were a Goth and on Halloween. Luckily for me, it was the latter. I could never pull off fishnets.

"I still haven't forgiven you for forgetting to bring me my energy drink the other day," I drawled, not impressed by his teasing.

"I'll make it up to you."

"You better."

Boone grinned and leaned down, pressing a kiss to my lips.

"That's a good start," I murmured.

I locked the door to the cottage behind me, and we made the three-minute walk over to Molly McCreedy's in silence. Mostly, I was annoyed Boone had gotten out of dressing up. I'd been conspiring for him to dress up as a fox ever since Mairead gave me the invitation, but he wouldn't have a bar of it. Sometimes, that man was too serious for his own good.

The party was in full swing as we approached the pub. Outside, Fergus's donkey was tied to her usual post with a blue tutu around her middle and a matching bow in her mane. Even she'd gotten the memo!

Carved pumpkins and hay bales were arranged outside, fake spider webs and skeletons were weaved around the exterior, and when we went inside, we were greeted by little old Mary Donnelly dressed as a pink fairy.

"Oh, Skye," she said when she saw my trench coat. "You're not dressed as a flasher, are you? There better be somethin' underneath there. No one wants to buy when you're giving away for free. I've still penciled you in for a spring reception at the teahouse. There's no way I'm writin' your bookin' in pen if you forgot to wear your underthings!"

My mouth fell open, and Boone began to laugh, his hands clutching his sides.

"And, Boone," she went on. "Where's your costume?" She clipped him around the ear, which silenced his amusement.

Shucking off my coat, I produced my shimmering green witches hat and shoved it onto my head.

"I'm not sure about that, but it's a sight better than what I was expectin'," Mary declared, before shooing us into the pub. "Have fun, dears."

"A witch?" Boone asked, cocking his head to the side. "Really?"

"Yes, really," I replied, dodging a skeleton hanging from the ceiling.

"Can I get you a drink?"

"Yes," I declared, swatting away a spider web. "A big one with one of those little umbrellas!"

As he disappeared toward the bar, I spotted Mairead twirling around on the dance floor by the fireplace. She was flirting with a boy I'd seen Mrs. Boyle chase with her broom on many occasions. I would go as far to say he was the old woman's number one nemesis before he'd disappeared off to college.

Wait… Mairead was *flirting*?

"Hey, Skye!"

Turning, I smiled as Maggie appeared. Her costume was a Bavarian Beer Maid. It seemed her irony meter was as high as mine.

"What are you wearin'?" she asked, tugging me on the arm.

"A brilliant costume," I declared.

"A sexy witch," she said with a laugh. "That's original."

"Hey, I'm Australian. We don't celebrate Halloween. Not really. I'm a newbie, thank you very much. I went for a costume classic." I put my hands on my hips and pouted seductively at her. "And I don't look half bad."

"Your skirt is so short I can almost see your knickers! I bet Boone likes it." She wiggled her eyebrows up and down.

"I'll let you know tomorrow." I winked suggestively.

"Lucky bitch," she said with a laugh as Sean McKinnon—who was dressed as a scarecrow with hay shoved underneath his rumpled clothes—wrapped his arm around her waist and twirled her away. "*Sean!*" she screeched. "What did I tell you about sexual harassment in the workplace!"

Boone appeared and handed me a drink with a smile, his free hand sliding around my waist.

"Maggie is right," he murmured into my ear. "I can almost see your knickers."

"I really think you should've come as a fox," I said. "Like a sports team mascot with an oversized fluffy head."

He screwed up his nose and sipped at his pint of beer. "That would've been ridiculous."

"More than a witch going to a costume party dressed as a witch?

"You have a point, but I'm not fallin' for one of your schemes."

"Schemes?" I gasped, pretending to be mortally wounded.

"Your scheme to make fun of me."

"*Never.*"

Smiling, I felt lighter than I had in days. This party was just what we needed to give us a break from the chaos that was being a Crescent Witch. One night without worry was heavenly. Maybe I would even get lucky downstairs by the end of it.

Glancing around the room, I sipped at my cider as I checked out all the costumes. Everyone had gone to a great deal of effort, even with Sean McKinnon's half-assed attempt at a scarecrow, and Boone's complete lack of being a pretend fox.

"Ah, there's Mark Ashlyn," Boone said. "I want to talk to him."

"Go," I said. "I'm a big girl."

He made a face and melted into the crowd. Setting my cider on a table, I looked for Maggie. Spying her across the pub, I laughed as I saw her dancing with Sean McKinnon, then twirling away and into Roy's arms. Cheeky old buggers.

A chill traveled down my spine, and I tensed, my gaze

meeting a pair of blue eyes. No, it couldn't be. My spidey sense was tingling to the point it felt like all my extremities had pins and needles.

Fae.

Focusing on the man, the air shimmered around him, and I sprang into action. Moving across the room, I zeroed in on the guy—a man I'd never seen before dressed in a leprechaun costume—and backed him into a corner.

"How dare you come here," I said, my voice low and full to bursting with a warning. "Give me one good reason why I shouldn't melt your brains out."

"You know why I'm here," he said, his eyes shimmering from human to fae. One second they were ordinary blue, then his entire eyeball was like iridescent crystal. Weirdo. "While you were enjoying the snow, *she returned*."

The snowstorm? Carman must've used the snow as a cover for her return to Ireland. That meant the ritual worked after all, and the fae before me... Deep fried shit on a stick! *He was a scout.*

My hand shot out, and I dug my fingers into his forearm. There was no way in hell I was letting him out of here alive, not when he'd been snooping and testing my defenses.

"Do you really want to use your magic in front of all these innocent humans?" he asked, his lip curling.

"Don't threaten me." I allowed a small sliver of magic to heat my hand. It got hotter and hotter until I could hear the sound of sizzling over the music.

The fae's expression twitched, giving away the fact he was in pain. I hoped he was stuck with my handprint seared into his flesh for eternity.

"There's nothing you can do, witch. All that awaits you is death."

"Then why don't you do something about it, huh? You could end this all right now."

The fae scowled, and I knew it had no power over me. The only thing that could end right now was him. I had a hold of it, and all it would take was a single thought to end its life.

I smirked and let it go. "You know what I can do, but that's not the half of it. That? That was an appetizer."

The fae cradled his arm against his chest and bared his pointy teeth at me.

"You're an attractive lot," I said, digging in the preverbal boot. "I'm guessing you're an Unseelie, aka a dark fairy. Desperate for power, desperate for fear, desperate to get through the doorways. Just all round desperate. You won't win. *Ever*. Stick that in your pipe and smoke it."

His eyes flared, and he tore through the crowd, practically breaking down the door as he went.

"What was that?" Boone asked, rushing to my side.

"Fae." I went after the pointy-toothed fairy, brushing aside a plastic skeleton and a stumbling Sean McKinnon as I went.

Outside, the street was empty, and I cursed.

"Why did I have to let him go?" I exclaimed as Boone prowled along the side of the road. "I had my hand on him." I could've held him for questioning…or something.

"You let him go?" Boone asked with a grimace.

"What was I supposed to do?" I exclaimed. "Melt him into a fairy puddle in front of the entire village? I know I'm wearing an ironic costume, but exposing the fact that I'm a witch would've been the worst thing I could've done." I let out a frustrated cry. It echoed along the empty road, the little hawthorn absorbing some of the magic I'd expelled along with it.

"Skye," Boone said warily. "What did he say to you?"

"The snowstorm the other week," I began, my heart filling with dread right up to the flood marker. "It was cover."

"Cover for what?" It came out uncertain like he already knew but didn't want to believe. Of course, he knew. Boone was clued up about these things. It couldn't be anyone else.

"Carman," I said. "Carman's in Ireland."

"*Cac*," he cursed. "The ritual…"

"I burned a calling card into that fairy's arm," I drawled, not wanting to think about the time I almost bled to death. "Did you see how he ran away from me? Let's see how she deals with that."

"You what?"

"I burned him with my magic." I was confused. "Wasn't I supposed to be able to do that?"

"I don't think so," he replied, staring down the road. "I don't think you were supposed to touch him at all."

"What makes you say that? I've touched fae before." Namely, the one who'd been impersonating my ex-boyfriend, Alex. "I've melted them into puddles of fairy juice."

"Because I didn't sense him," Boone said. "Not at all. To me, he was human. He must've had some kind of barrier spell…one you burned right through."

I held up my hand and stared at it. Did this have something to do with the purple monkey typewriter? I was doing something I hadn't been able to do before, and the only thing that had changed was the bump on the head I'd gotten while trying to unlock Boone's memories. What if

I'd broken something? Carman was back after a thousand years of exile, and I was broken.

Suddenly, I felt extremely foolish in my sexy witch costume.

Happy Halloween.

CHAPTER 8

"Elephant, rose water, pineapple, toaster!"

I sat up in bed, my chest heaving. I swiped at the sweat on my forehead and dabbed my nightie against the perspiration under my boobs.

Outside, the night was darker than usual. There was no moonlight streaming through the windows to lighten the little bedroom, so I reached over and turned on the lamp. Warm light lit up the shadows, and I placed a hand on the empty bed beside me.

Another dream? And here I was hoping it was just concussion talking.

There was something… A feeling of dread? I was at the pineapple, and an elephant was inside the toaster. When I touched it, rose water came out. That was the stupidest thing I'd ever heard. An elephant in a toaster!

Scratching my head, I reached for my tarot cards. The feel of them was comforting as I shuffled, and my thoughts went to Aileen. What would she do if she were here? It was hard to know since I never really knew her. Boone was the only other person who knew her as a witch.

A shiver went down my spine as I dwelled on what we'd found at the clearing. Nothing. Only a few months had passed since her death, but the ground where Hannah had dragged her under was unbroken.

My mother, my father, my life back in Australia. I'd lost it all, but I'd gained so much through the Crescent Calling. Knowing Carman was back in Ireland was a weight on my shoulders I never thought I would have the moment I'd seen Boone turn into a fox for the first time.

Drawing a card from the tarot deck, I sighed when I saw the Chariot reversed. *Again.*

"I already know," I told the card. "Stop beating it into my head."

Glancing over at the window, I felt a bad case of the heebie-jeebies tingling across my exposed skin, and I leaped out of bed and yanked down the blind. Some fae had wings, right? What if they flew up and perved at me while I slept? I shook out my limbs, my paranoia rising.

We'd known Carman might come all along, but now that she was here, I didn't know what to do. Everything I'd learned about being a Crescent Witch had dissolved into mush.

Curling up under the quilt, I left the lamp on and let my senses fly around the cottage. I felt Mairead asleep in the spare bedroom and a few nighttime creatures scurrying around in the forest, but nothing else stirred. There were no flying fairies or ancient witches gearing up for a grudge match.

There was nothing at all.

When the next morning dawned, I moved to the couch downstairs with a can of energy drink and the Crescent spell book. Another night of zero sleep, and I was a zombie.

I heard the front door opening, and I called out, "That better be you, Boone. If not…I love a *barbecue!*"

"But only if I cook it, right?" Boone leaned against the doorframe, looking handsome in his leather bomber jacket and boots.

"Thank, God," I declared. "I don't like charcoal."

"I better light the fire for you, then. I don't what you burnin' down the cottage."

"Thanks."

He crossed the room and began fussing over the fire, laying out logs and kindling in an elaborate teepee design that had me wondering if he was an arsonist in his secret forgotten life. He had a certain *je ne sais quoi* with hot things.

"Where's Mairead?" he asked, lighting a match.

"She went Christmas shopping in Sligo," I replied. "Took the bus an hour ago."

"You're not openin' Irish Moon today?"

"Nope." I shook my head. "We needed a break."

"Everythin' okay?" He nodded toward the six-pack of energy drinks on the coffee table.

It was no use brushing it off, so I told him. "I had another dream last night."

Boone raised his head from the fireplace, and his brow creased.

I shrugged. "I know it was important, but whenever I think about it, all I get is nonsense."

"So it wasn't the knock on the head?"

"No. At least, I don't think so." I stroked the page of

the spell book idly, my brain fogging up as I tried to recall what was just out of my grasp. "I can't help thinking it's another witchy omen."

"Like what?"

"Like something is warning me about Carman and her plans. Like when the hawthorn warned me about Lucy."

"Skye, the hawthorn put you in a vision of your family bein' burned alive. You were tied to a stake."

"So?" It was my turn to frown.

"It's not a nice way of warnin' you, is all."

"Well, it's either that or I'm broken. Broken would be bad."

"You're not broken." Boone rose to his feet and dusted off his hands. "Your magic is still growin'. You said it yourself. Maybe it's a reaction to Carman returnin'."

"Like I've been given growth hormones?" I raised my eyebrows and clutched the spell book against my chest. "Okay…"

"All we can do is wait and watch," he said. "Enjoy Christmas, Skye. You need moments like these."

"To make the impending doom less doomy?" I rolled my eyes.

I couldn't stop thinking about all the witches out there who might be falling victim to Carman's insatiable thirst for power. She might be hoovering up a poor witch's magic as we spoke about hiding out in Derrydun and waiting for her to come to us…at her full strength.

"We can't leave the hawthorn unguarded," Boone said, reading my expression.

"Are you sure you're not a telepath?"

"I'm sure."

Sure felt like he was.

"If there were more Crescents, then maybe we

could've planned to go after her," Boone went on. "But you're all there is."

Thinking about the Nightshade Witches, I knew finding allies would be impossible. To the other witches, I was the problem, and knowing Carman was back would only make things worse. Add a dash of taking away a whole coven's Legacy forever—I understood why Legacy was capitalized now—and you had the perfect recipe for hatred. Long story short, I was screwed.

"They know we're here…" I murmured.

Boone frowned.

"I can use my magic more openly," I said. "I can cast barriers and wards or something around the village and the hawthorn. I can do something."

"You'll attract wanderin' craglorn," Boone pointed out. "They'll sense your magic and—"

"Go poof!" I exclaimed, clapping my hands together.

"I don't think a barrier is like an electric fence, Skye."

"Don't dash my hopes for a Christmas miracle," I said with a pout.

"Talkin' about Christmas miracles. I've got a surprise for you."

My ears pricked up at the word surprise. Thankful for the distraction, I shot to my feet and dropped the spell book on the couch.

"Oh! Oh! What is it? A pony?"

Boone's eyebrows quirked. "Uh, no?"

My shoulders sank, and I screwed up my nose.

"Just…" He sighed and gestured for me to stay put. "Wait here."

"One Christmas miracle, two Christmas miracle…"

There was rustling and thumping at the front door, then the tip of a pine tree was poking into the lounge room. I could've made a dirty joke, but I held my tongue when I saw how excited Boone was.

"A Christmas tree?" I asked.

I'd never had a tree after I'd moved out of home. It always seemed like too much work with all the putting up and taking down and the tangled tinsel. Not to mention there was always one light that didn't work, and when one bulb blew, the whole strand was useless. Who kept the spares, anyway? You put them in a place so safe you forgot where a year later when it was time to get them out again.

The room filled with the scent of pine as Boone set up the tree in the corner, needles falling everywhere as he steadied the base.

"What are we decorating it with?" I asked, watching him. "Miniature athames, wands, and pentagrams?"

"Very funny," he said, going outside and bringing back a box. "I got all kinds of stuff." He pulled packets of ornaments and wads of tinsel out and strew them all over the floor. "Baubles, tinsel, lights…"

"I see there's a color scheme," I declared, holding up a box of black, silver, and gold Christmas balls. I snickered as a dirty thought lit up my brain. *Balls.*

"It's a Crescent tree."

I raised my eyebrows. A Crescent tree, huh? Diving back into the box, I found a packet of crescent moon ornaments and snorted. Merry Crescent-mas.

Opening the plastic package, I held up one of the little moons and hooked it onto the tree. Boone smiled up at me, knowing how better I felt even before I did.

"Thanks," I said. "You're right as usual."

His smile turned into a grin. "You're welcome."

Christmas morning was a whirlwind of activity at the cottage.

We all sat underneath the horror that was the Christmas tree I'd decorated and unwrapped our meager presents. With everything that had happened since Halloween, I hadn't thought about let alone had time to go get any presents, so I did last-minute shopping online with express delivery.

Boone was still stuck in Derrydun, unwilling to go past the limits of the hawthorns out of habit, so he shopped locally like the good guy he was. He'd given me a new pair of fingerless gloves and a sloppy beanie he'd asked Cheese Wheel Aoife from the handicrafts store to knit. Black with metallic gold thread weaved through. Very Crescent of him.

I'd been a total smartass and given him a new black and red checkered shirt and a black T-shirt with a fox design on the front. For Mairead, I gave her a new pair of Doc Martins, and Boone got her a fancy box to put all her paints in.

But Mairead blew us all out of the water.

Hanging in the hallway was the painting of Derrydun she'd been working on for the last two months. All that building up of color and dabbing blots of paint all over the canvas had really paid off. The finished product was stunning with all its intricate details. The tower house stood proudly on the hill, each block of stone detailed with the very tip of her paintbrush. The sky was streaked with swirling clouds, the forest below was awash with every shade of green imaginable, and the main street of the village was vibrant and alive. The hot pink of Mary's Teahouse stood out like a sore thumb among it all, but that was exactly how it was like in real life. *Garish.* She'd even managed to get the ancient hawthorn in the picture. Its canopy rose over the rest of the trees in the forest, tall and proud. The kid had mad skills.

Once the presents were open, Boone and I showered and dressed before making our way over to Molly McCreedy's. Apparently, Christmas lunch at the pub was a huge tradition in Derrydun. Everyone came, bringing food, drink, and presents, and partied until they were drunk as skunks. It was the local Irish way, Boone said. The village was so tight-knit that everyone was everyone's family, and no one was turned away.

I didn't have any presents, so I brought along all kinds of crystals and tumbled stones, handing them out to those whose energy matched. Amethyst for Mrs. Boyle. Citrine for Mary Donnelly. Rose quartz for Roy, and even though it was pink, it was good for his nature-loving soul. Even Sean McKinnon got a piece of tiger's eye. He grumbled about getting a rock but put it into his pocket, anyway.

"Skye! Skye!"

I turned at the sound of Mairead's excited voice and stumbled as she almost crashed into me. She was wearing her usual drab garb, but she'd donned a black Santa hat with white furry trim. I'd known her long enough to not be surprised by the irony.

"Where's the fire?" I asked, holding her back.

"You'll never guess what happened!"

"Mairead… You're…" I made a face. "*Happy*."

"So?"

"Aren't Goths meant to be mopey?"

"*Pfft*." She rolled her eyes. "That's a stereotype."

"Are you sure? Because when you wear black lipstick and smile—"

"I made up with me parents," she blurted.

"Huh?" When did that happen? I was such a good guardian—forgetting to make sure she wasn't getting high on paint fumes, feeding her microwave meals, making her do her own laundry, and not even knowing what was going on in her life. Superb parenting.

"They want me to come home," she went on. "For Christmas, then…" She shrugged. "I gave them a paintin' I did. The one of the gyrfalcon in the hawthorn tree outside of Irish Moon."

"You did another painting?" I frowned. "Man, I'm such a bad parent."

"No, you're pretty cool."

"So you're moving back?"

She nodded. "They are me parents… Even though they kicked me out."

"As long as they don't try to force you to go back to Trinity."

Mairead shrugged. "I don't think they understood about me art. Now they've seen, I guess they came around. They were disappointed about how I came home…"

I nodded. She couldn't exactly tell them about being kidnapped by evil fae who mistook her for me, could she? She hadn't been happy at Trinity, but being snatched off the street had ultimately pushed her into coming back to Derrydun.

"Do they still think I'm the devil incarnate?" I asked, my lips quirking.

She grinned and backed away, weaving between Mary Donnelly and Cheese Wheel Aoife before using Mrs. Boyle as a buffer.

"*Mairead!*" I stamped my foot. "Don't you walk away from me, young lady!"

"What's going on?" Boone asked, appearing beside me.

"Mairead's moving out."

"Well, you did ask for a Christmas miracle."

I gasped and slapped him on the arm.

"*Ow.*" He rubbed his bicep.

"I'm glad they made up. It was an awful side effect of her kidnapping."

"See, Skye? Everythin' is starting to work out." Boone smiled and guided me to a spot he'd saved for us at the table by the fireplace.

Sliding into a chair, I fiddled with the cutlery as food started to appear. Maggie moved from table to table, laying out platters and jugs. Even Sean McKinnon was giving her a hand and walking more steadily than usual.

"Is Sean…sober?" I asked, leaning toward Boone.

"See?" he said with a wink. "Christmas brings out the best in everyone."

I glanced around the pub, taking in everyone's smiling faces. Roy was wearing a paper hat from the inside of a Christmas cracker. Mary Donnelly was decked out in pink and completely sloshed on mulled wine. Maggie was still flitting between tables, topping up beer glasses and ferrying out bowls of mushy peas. Mairead was sitting between her parents, looking pleased as punch, her black fuzzy Santa hat askew on her head. Fergus was feeding his dog scraps under the table. Even Mrs. Boyle looked as if she had a smile on her face.

An overwhelming pang of despair came over me at the thought of what was coming. How was I supposed to protect them from Carman? If she managed to take the hawthorn and open the doorway… The thought of what might come out of there was the stuff of nightmares. An army of fae just like the scout who'd threatened me at Halloween. Derrydun wouldn't stand a chance.

"Skye." Boone placed his hand on my thigh under the table and squeezed. "Don't dwell on what-ifs."

"I just…" I trailed off, knowing anything I said would sound lame. I was supposed to be the strong one. I was the last Crescent Witch, the sole member of the most badass coven there ever was. I was meant to know what to do. Watching and waiting didn't seem like the Crescent thing to do.

"Ever since the craglorn, you've been stressin'," he murmured into my ear. "We can only do what's in our power."

"You sound like a broken record," I drawled.

"Life's too short," he murmured. Picking up his glass, he stood and bashed the side with his fork. *Ding, ding, ding.*

"What are you doing?" I said with a hiss, glancing around uneasily.

"Can I have your attention," he called out to the room. "I've got somethin' important to say."

I tugged on his shirt as the din faded to curious murmurings. Mary Donnelly caught my gaze and gave me an enthusiastic thumbs up. All eyes turned our way, and I tugged at Boone more furiously.

"Sit down," I whispered, trying to smile and glare at the same time. I must've looked frightening, especially since I was flushed red with embarrassment. "You can't tell them…"

But Boone wasn't listening. I was full-on ready to whoop his ass if he began changing into a silver fox when he started talking. Boone *talking*? I'd always taken him for 'the silent and in the corner' type, not a public speaker.

"Seven months ago, this curious Australian with her smart mouth and uncanny resemblance to her late mother, Aileen, landed in our laps quite unexpectedly. In that seven months, there've been untold amounts of chaos, excitement, and scandal," he said.

"Hear, hear!" Roy bellowed, stamping his foot on the ground much to the amusement of the villagers.

"She's filled me life with excitement, countless pop culture references that go straight over me head, frightful danger, and unwaverin' support, and a smack on the back of me head when I'm throwin' a tantrum. That's why I can't bear to be apart from her another day." Boone turned to me and lowered himself to one knee. "Skye Williams…" He fished about in his pocket—while I tried to get my heart to start beating again—and produced a silver and gold ring. "*An bpósfaidh tú mé?*" Then in English, he said, "Will ye marry me?"

I dropped my fork, and it clattered to the floor. Fergus's Jack Russell darted under the table and began gnawing at the choice bit of roast beef I'd been about to put into my mouth when Boone had stood.

"Skye?" he asked hesitantly.

"*Yes!*" I shrieked, almost falling off my chair.

"I told you," Mary said to Roy. "Spring."

Boone grasped my face in his hands and kissed me hard. "*Cac*, I almost didn't think you'd say yes…"

"Put it on," I demanded. "It isn't real until the ring is on."

"Is that true?"

"Dunno, but it sounds like the official thing to do." I held out my hand and wiggled my fingers.

"Like I said," Boone murmured, sliding the silver and gold ring on. "*Untold amounts of chaos.*"

"I'll agree with the chaos but untold amounts?" I made a face. "I'm disputing that."

Abruptly, Sean shot to his feet and exclaimed, "Maggie!"

The entire pub fell silent as he leaped around the table and knelt at Maggie's feet.

"Sean, you're makin' a scene," she said through her teeth. "You're stealin' Boone's moment, you eejit!"

"I love you, Maggie!" he exclaimed, clutching at her legs. "I've been fightin' it for so long, but it's time!"

Roy snorted, earning himself a kick from Mary under the table. The cutlery jingled, and beer sloshed from the old farmer's pint glass.

Maggie shot me a look that said 'help,' and I rose to my feet.

"Sean McKinnon!" I exclaimed. "I always thought you were a gentleman."

He stared at me, looking vacant, blinked twice, then let Maggie go.

"Even when you were calling me a witch," I added, much to the everyone's amusement.

"You've got to know when a woman doesn't want your attention, boy," Roy bellowed. "*Go dtachta grá leatromach do bhall fearga!*"

The entire pub burst out into riotous laughter, but as usual, I had no clue what any of it meant. Leaning over to Boone, I opened my mouth to ask him, but his seat was empty.

He was gone.

CHAPTER 9

It was freezing outside.

I huddled into my jacket and shoved my gloved hands into my pockets as deep as they could go. My breath vaporized in plumes as I glanced up and down the darkening street. The wool Cheese Wheel Aoife had knitted the gloves in was soft against my skin, and the matching beanie was toasty over my delicate ears.

It wasn't like Boone to disappear like he had. Not after asking me to marry him in front of the whole village. I hoped everything was okay, and he wasn't outside hyperventilating, but I couldn't take any chances. There were too many magical unknowns hanging over our heads for me not to go and check.

"Boone?" I called, my voice coming out softer than I'd intended.

Great, I was freaking out like the heroine in a horror movie.

I took a step forward into the twilight. The days had become shorter and shorter the more winter had set in, and it got full-on dark at four p.m. It was madness. Did the sun set that early in Australia? I hardly remembered.

After a second, I sensed Boone further down the road. Sighing in relief, I stepped forward with more confidence. He was under the hawthorn, but I didn't get far when I realized he wasn't alone.

He was talking to another man who looked a lot like him. Tall, scruffy, dark hair, leather jacket, big boots. It could be his twin, but I'd never seen the guy before in my life. He was a stranger, and it only meant one thing. *Stranger danger.*

My immediate reaction was to launch into action and blast the guy with my magic, but something told me to stop. *Stop, wait, listen.* I felt an unknown force tugging me backward like little hands grasping at my jacket. Glancing down, there was nothing there, but I heeded the warning, anyway.

Ducking back behind the cover of Molly McCreedy's, I steadied my breathing and cast out my hearing.

"It's me. *Dub*," the man said in a thick Irish accent.

"I don't know you," Boone said, his voice full of doubt.

"Of course, you don't, but you did."

"All I know is that you've got one eye," Boone said, his voice sounding more like a growl with every word he spoke. "And I know a wolf who lost an eye…"

The man—who seemed to be called Dub—sighed and threw his hands into the air. "You always had the power to unlock your memories, Dain. She took them for your own good, you know."

"What are you talkin' about? Who took them?" Boone stepped forward and grasped the lapels of the man's coat and almost lifted him clear off the ground. "You better start answerin' before I rip your head off."

"You'd like that, wouldn't you?" Dub shoved Boone back and dusted off his coat.

"I can sense the magic in you, shapeshifter. Start explainin' or…"

"Or your little Crescent will come out here and smack me ass?" Dub laughed and thumped Boone on the shoulder. "Unlikely. We're under the hawthorn for starters. She wouldn't risk damagin' it."

"She's got a good aim."

Damn right, I did.

"I've had enough of your smart mouth." The man was getting more exasperated as their conversation went on. "She's going to be so mad at me for this."

I felt the burst of magic before Boone did. Even with the hawthorn shielding them, the wave washed over me like sludge, weighing down my limbs. *Wait, a shapeshifter couldn't use magic like that.*

Boone gasped and clutched his head, his eyes widening.

"What did you do?" he exclaimed.

"What you were too cowardly to," Dub said with a sneer. "You were always the runt of the litter."

"No, no, no," Boone murmured, looking distraught. "I can't… *She can't…*"

"Dain," he said, placing a hand on Boone's shoulder. "It's time to come home. Mother is waiting for you."

"Mother?"

"Think about it," Dub said with a sneer. "Think about it real hard."

"*Carman.*"

I gasped. Slapping a hand over my mouth, I darted back around the corner and held my breath as my heart slammed into the wall of my chest cavity.

Boone's forgotten identity! He was Carman's son? She'd locked away his memories and sent his brothers after him. Why? Was it all an elaborate trick to get to Aileen and me?

I didn't know, but it explained a great deal. Boone wasn't just a shapeshifter. He was half witch. The things he'd known I'd attributed to Aileen teaching him, but what if he knew because of his own forgotten witch Legacy? Suddenly, the ring he'd given me moments before felt heavy on my finger. Marriage, love, loyalty. Those things seemed like nothing compared to this.

"She's forgiven you for your indiscretion, Dain," Dub went on. "You're fighting on the wrong side, little brother. You belong with us."

Boone's brother. Oh, shite! Carman's three sons… I wanted to puke. There was another one. Three shapeshifting wolves with witch abilities. The mountain I had to climb was growing, and the odds were piling up against little old me. Boone… What was he going to do now that he knew?

I'd said it didn't matter who he'd been all this time, but it did. It did matter. Boone was the son of the enemy.

Wiping away a big fat tear that had rolled down my cheek, I slipped back into the pub and plastered a fake smile on my face.

"Where'd Boone disappear to?" Maggie asked as I pulled off my gloves and hat.

"I think it hit him," I replied.

"What?"

"What he just got himself into. He's outside contemplating the rest of his life hitched to me."

"Oh, it's not that bad. He's lucky to have you if you ask me. Besides, Boone is a catch and a half."

I smiled, but the light didn't reach my eyes. *If she only knew the truth.*

Sitting back down at the table, I went on like nothing had happened. I let Mary Donnelly prattle on about her plans for the wedding in one ear while Sean McKinnon grumbled in the other about taking away his best mate. *If only they knew the truth, too.*

My heart was dissolving the longer I sat there alone, waiting for the man I was supposedly going to marry to return. What if he didn't? Maybe he'd already run off with his long-lost brother to join his thousand-year-old mother as a soldier in her plot to destroy the world. I didn't want to acknowledge the fact that Boone might be right up there in the age department, either.

I was a clueless little witch, and he was—

"Are you okay?"

My heart twisted in fright as Boone sat next to me. His cheeks were flushed with the cold, and the longer I stared at him, the more my anxiety rose.

"Skye?" His forehead crease deepened.

It was then I realized he wasn't going to tell me. He was going to keep his identity a secret. Either he was still reconciling the fact his mum was a crazy, psychopathic, power hungry bitch or he'd decided to play both sides. Or just this one. He was in a prime position being all naked in my bed five nights a week…and now he was engaged to the last witch standing in Carman's way.

Oh, hell, what was I supposed to do?

"Yeah," I replied. "Yeah."

"I should ask you to marry me every day," he said with a smile. "It's the only time I've ever seen you lost for words."

"Yeah," I said again. *Lame.*

"You do want this?" he asked, his grin fading.

"Of course, I do." *With the Boone who had amnesia.* "I

don't know anyone else who'd be crazy enough to marry me." Reaching for the plum pudding, I dished a slice each into our empty bowls. "Here. No Christmas feast is over until the pudding is gone."

"Is that an Australian thing?"

"No," I said, putting on my best 'everything is going to be okay' mask. "It's a Skye thing."

CHAPTER 10

I hadn't even looked at the ring Boone had given me at Christmas. Not really.

I wore it every day, knew it was gold and silver, but if anyone asked me about the design, I couldn't tell them what it was. All I could see when I stared at him was Carman. He didn't have her coloring, but his eyes could be hers. I'd only met her once in the vision she'd pulled me into—the one with the creepy doors that opened endlessly in the same room—but I would never forget her face. She was a ginger minge. Minge being slang for female pubic hair.

The point was, Boone must take after his father. Whoever that was.

Two days before New Year, I sat behind the counter at Irish Moon, the laptop in front of me, a Goth girl uploading photographs, and the tarot card that had been the bane of my existence since the ritual—the Chariot —beside me.

While Mairead chattered happily about moving back home and her trip to Belfast for New Year's Eve, I wallowed in the pit of my own misery. She couldn't stop talking about the alternative pub she was going to—a place called Voodoo where all the Goths, punks, and rockers hung out—with some new friends she'd made online. After giving her a stern talking to about stranger danger and who and who not to let into her hotel room, we went back to listing crystals on the Irish Moon online store.

Maybe if I meditated on the tarot card, it might be able to reveal something else to me. Something I'd obviously missed. Had there been clues? Obviously, Boone's new wolf shape was a glaring indicator, and the fact his mind didn't want me to break open the barrier keeping his memories locked up. Had I been that blind?

I'd believed the Chariot had been forewarning about Carman's return but in hindsight…

The bell above the door rang, and I froze as Boone walked in. He stomped his boots on the mat before crossing the shop floor and leaning against the counter. He just stood there, all comfortable and handsome like he hadn't just found out his secret past was the bombshell of the century. I couldn't handle it.

"What are you doing here?" I asked, the question coming out a little more forcibly than I'd intended.

"I've finished up at Roy's, and I'm free for lunch before I have to be at Molly McCreedy's," he said with a frown. "Do you want to go to Mary's for somethin' to eat?"

"I'm not hungry," I muttered, looking at the tarot card.

I sensed Mairead's scowl burning into the side of my face.

"Skye?"

I glanced up at Boone, my heart twisting to the point I wasn't sure there was any blood left in it.

"Can we go outside?" he asked, nodding toward the door.

"Please, do," Mairead declared. "I don't want to go out there again while you have secret conversations. It's freezin'."

"Fine." My lip curled, and I stood, dropping the tarot card.

Picking up my jacket, I shoved my arms into it as I strode outside. We had to have the talk sooner or later, and I had a terrible poker face. Keeping my witchy abilities from the village was different. I wasn't hurting anyone because my mission in life was to protect, but this... *Cac. Cac-itty McCac!*

Boone closed the shop door behind him as the cold bit into my exposed fingers. I couldn't even bring myself to wear the gloves he'd given me.

Pressing my palm against my forehead, I was sure I was burning up. I felt sick. I wasn't going to faint, was I? Maybe if I puked, it would freeze solid on the footpath. I breathed out a plume of vaporized air.

"Skye, you've been... Ever since Christmas when I asked you to marry me..." Boone shoved a hand through his unruly hair. "It was too soon, wasn't it? I just thought, with everythin' that's going on..." He trailed off and glanced at the hawthorn. *The scene of the crime.*

"That we better have our white picket fence moment before we all die?" I felt like slapping him with my magic. I wanted to be happy. I wanted to marry him, but not like this. Not when he couldn't tell me the truth. Not when I didn't know whose side he was on.

Looking over my shoulder, I spotted Mairead staring at us through the window. Grabbing Boone's arm, I dragged him down the lane and behind the shop.

"Skye…" he said, dragging his heels. "What's goin' on?"

The longer he was here, the riskier it became. Super-creepy one-eyed Dub may have unlocked his memories, but who knew what else he'd done. Boone was half witch, that much was clear. Now he knew he had magic of his own, and possibly had a billion years to master it, there was no telling what he could do.

I didn't want to admit it, but I didn't trust him. The man I loved and wanted to marry. *I didn't trust him.*

The only place I felt safe was at the ancient hawthorn even though it was the exact spot his mother wanted to get to. If I stood with the hawthorn and called on the Crescent ancestors, maybe his true intentions would be revealed. That was if those pesky spirits showed up in the first place. They were the definition of unreliable.

The forest felt charged like something forbidden had walked into it. It was a strange sensation like awareness had brought some ancient defense mechanism to life.

Boone didn't say anything as I led him down the path toward the clearing. His mood was sour, but mine was worse. My magic was flaring hotter with each step. He would have to sense it and wonder what had me so worked up. *Dammit*, now I was overthinking everything. I was a doer, usually, not a worrywart.

Stepping into the clearing, I let go of Boone's arm and approached the hawthorn. Placing my hand on its trunk, I closed my eyes, but all I felt was scratchy bark underneath my palm.

"Skye? Why are we here?"

C'mon, I pleaded. *I need you. Please…*

"Skye?"

"I can't do this…" I turned, knowing I was in this on

my own. *As usual.* Is this what betrayal felt like? Complete and total abandonment? Without Boone, I was alone, and Mairead… Mairead couldn't help. It was selfish to even ask after what she'd been through because of me.

"Can't do what? Marry me?"

"I saw you," I blurted, unable to hold it in anymore. "*I saw you.*"

All the color drained from Boone's cheeks, and he stood there like a lump, staring at me in shock. I was a Crescent Witch, the last of the most badass coven there ever was, so of course, I would find out. I wished he would wipe that dumb look off his face.

"Were you ever going to tell me?" I whispered, fighting back tears.

"I don't know."

I shook my head, my thoughts jumbled.

"If I'd known…"

"If you'd known, then what?" I demanded. "Pretended you cared? Went on playing the secret agent?"

"No!"

"Why were you being chased by your brothers the night you came to Derrydun? Why did she take your memories?"

Boone's jaw tightened, and he didn't say anything. He knew all his buried secrets now, but he was conspicuously tight-lipped about what they revealed. It only solidified his guilt in my mind.

"Was it all an elaborate scam to get to the Crescent Witches?" I demanded. "You got Aileen killed, and now you're—"

"It wasn't me fault," he declared. "*It wasn't me fault.* Carman wanted me, too."

"Yeah, because you're her kid, Boone. Is she using you, or was it your idea?"

He shook his head like his headaches were piercing his brain.

"When Aileen told you she had a daughter, did you decide to stay so you could worm your way into my life?"

"If that were true, then why did I stop the ritual?" he asked thinly. "Why was there a block on me memories? You felt it, Skye."

"The ritual that was stopped *too late*," I scoffed and shook my head. "The block pushed me away when I tried to break it open. You didn't want me in there."

"*What?*"

"And when she came, which side were you going to fight on?" It took all my strength, but I glanced up and met his gaze. "Hers or mine?"

"Skye, you've got to understand. I didn't know who I was."

"And you do now," I snapped. "You're Carman's *son*."

"I can't help who I am!" he roared.

"And neither can I."

"So this is it?" he asked. "You're drawin' a battle line between us?"

"I have to. You weren't going to tell me, Boone." Before he could open his mouth to argue, I added, "Don't deny it. How could I trust you now?"

"You said it didn't matter," he whispered, clenching his fists. "You said it didn't matter who I was before."

"That was before I found out you're the son of the woman who wants to kill me and destroy the world. The son who was part of…" I choked on the truth, my throat burning with unshed tears. "How many witches did you kill?"

Boone stared at me, his expression giving away everything. Countless. That was his unspoken answer. *Countless.*

"She's in Ireland," I said, staring past him. "You can go home now. You can go back to where you belong."

With Boone at Carman's side, she would know exactly how powerful I was, how I would react, and all the tricks I'd learned to master my magic. I was screwed. Utterly, completely, up shit creek without a paddle. I couldn't kill him, so I had to let him go. I loved him.

Boone was still in there, and Dain… I didn't know who Dain was, but he was in control now.

"Skye…"

"What could you possibly say to make this better?" I demanded. "*What?*"

"Nothing," he replied. "I did bad things back then. I…" He glanced up at the hawthorn, his face twisted in pain. "I don't belong there, and I never belonged here. Where do I go?"

"Away," I snapped, not wanting to hear his broody nonsense.

Turning my back on him, I placed my hand on the ancient hawthorn. There was an opening here someplace, but even I didn't know how to access it let alone unlock the binding keeping it shut. All of this heartache for a little door.

"I was home…" Boone murmured. "I wish… I wish I'd forgotten forever."

When I finally had the courage to turn around, he was gone.

CHAPTER 11

I'd fallen in love with the enemy.

Playing with the talisman I'd made back in summer, I sighed. After Boone had left, I went home and retrieved it from the jewelry box on the nightstand in my room. Then I'd gone outside, intending on going back to Irish Moon, but I hadn't made it past the carrot patch. There weren't any carrots in it this time of year, so I was basically sitting in the dirt. *Freak.*

Without Boone... Without his love and companionship, how was I meant to go on?

Turning over the little golden crystal, I studied the facets and blemishes. The protective barrier was still active, maybe a little duller than before, but it was still there.

"Skye?"

I glanced up at the sound of Mairead's voice. She was standing over me, looking like a ginormous thundercloud.

"Were you comin' back to the shop?" she demanded. "Or were you just goin' to leave me there like an eejit?"

I shrugged, the numbness spreading. It was becoming

harder and harder to differentiate between the heartbreak and the cold.

The Goth girl's angry expression faded. "What's wrong? Why are you sittin' in the dirt?"

I'd been so callous. With the Nightshade Witches and with Boone. I saw it now. Why people hated the Crescents. We were cold-hearted bitches who cared for nothing but our Legacy. I was arrogant in the worst possible way.

"Boone's gone," I said, clutching the talisman.

"What do you mean?" Mairead knelt beside me, the spot between her eyebrows knitted together so tight that she almost had a monobrow.

"He's gone."

"Where?"

I began to shake, the gravity of what had just happened out in the forest catching up with me.

"Skye… You're wearin' your crystal again…" She uncurled my fingers and pried the little spear of quartz from my grasp.

I snatched it back, never wanting to let my shield go. It helped me with the sluagh, so it would help me now.

Mairead frowned and sat in the first row next to me. "You're really scarin' me…"

Glancing at her, I knew I had a duty even though I felt like imploding. I was supposed to be a good role model and a protector of magic. Not a self-absorbed wallower in a carrot patch.

"You said Carman had three sons," I began, gathering the first pieces of my shattered heart. "Boone… He's one of them."

"Huh?" Mairead's mouth fell open.

I explained it to her in as few words as possible. How his brother was the one-eyed wolf, how he showed up on

Christmas and unlocked Boone's memories, and how Boone wasn't going to tell me the truth. Every explanation that came out of my mouth felt like I was choking on razor blades.

"Maybe he was goin' to tell you," she said. "Maybe he just needed time."

"It's not that simple, Mairead!" I exclaimed. "When his memories came back, so did everything else. Who he was, who he is… Boone was just a person who stepped in to compensate for his lack of knowledge. Dain is back in control now, and Dain the wolf has gone back to his mummy."

"Dain, the enemy you mean."

I nodded.

Mairead pouted, looking like she was mad at me.

"Don't look at me like that!" I exclaimed. "I loved him, Mairead. I was going to marry him! Don't you understand what betrayal is?"

She nodded, glancing at the dirt beneath us. "I understand, Skye. I'm not a moody teenager anymore. I know about these things. You want to know what I think?"

I didn't really want to hear anything, but I knew she was going to tell me one way or another.

"All this time he was in Derrydun, he didn't know. Carman took away his memories, but what if the Boone we knew was always who he was?"

I didn't want to admit she was right, but it was too late for second chances and righting wrongs. Carman was in Ireland, and she was coming. With Boone or without him.

"You're making it worse," I muttered.

Mairead leaned her head against my shoulder. "You still have me."

For once in my life, I was out of smartass comebacks.

"Thanks," I said, debating on whether or not I should tell her about the snowstorm that heralded Carman's homecoming. Shaking my head, I decided not to and rose to my feet.

"Where are you goin'?" the Goth girl asked, mirroring my movement.

"To microwave some dinner. Want some?"

She screwed up her nose. "Nah ah."

"Good, I only have one left."

Mairead pouted and walked back toward the main street, her boots clomping in the snow. It wasn't fair to dump all my magical poop into her human lap. This was a fight I had to face alone. As a witch and as a descendant of the Crescents who had gotten me into this mess in the first place.

Sighing, I walked toward the cottage, knowing my ass was completely caked in mud and soaked through to my undies.

"Skye?" Mairead called out.

I glanced over my shoulder and found her standing at the edge of the garden, looking worried.

"Are you sure you're goin' to be okay?"

"I have to be," I replied. "The world doesn't stop spinning for one broken heart."

It was New Year's Day when I finally got out of bed and put on some normal people clothes. My *Teenage Mutant Ninja Turtles* pajamas were starting to stink, and I was almost sure I'd forgotten how to walk. If it weren't for my bodily functions, I wouldn't have gotten up at all.

After seeing Boone almost every single day since I'd arrived in Derrydun, his absence was like a tear in the space-time continuum. It was unnatural and wrong, but I had to keep reminding myself who he was. Who or what? I wasn't sure which of those two words to put into that statement.

Molly McCreey's was a bubble of warmth as I entered.

The fire was roaring in the hearth, and a dozen villagers huddled around it. Sean McKinnon sat by the bar, nursing a pint of beer, his woolly jumper looking ratty and worn, and the scruff on his face not faring any better. He looked like he had a broken heart, but that wasn't anything new. Ever since his wife died, he'd been in mourning, but at Christmas, he'd made a declaration of love at Maggie's feet. Seeing him now, I wasn't sure who he was pining over anymore.

When he turned and saw me approaching the bar, his eyes lit up and not in a welcoming way. It was as if my presence had stoked the fires of Hell.

"Hey, Skye," Maggie said. "You don't look so good. Are you feelin' okay?"

I glanced at Sean, whose scowl deepened. Either he knew or he had latent magical talent. He was always calling me a witch like he knew something everyone else didn't, but I was sure it had more to do with being Boone's best friend than anything supernatural.

"Boone's gone," Sean declared, erupting like a volcano. "He hasn't shown up to work in three days. I've had double the work on the farm, chasin' eejit sheep across the hill and slippin' over in piles of shit. Want to know why?"

"Three days?" Maggie asked, ignoring his rant. "That's not like him. He's supposed to work the kitchen tonight."

"The last time this happened, it was because of her." The farmer jabbed an accusing finger at me.

Anger welled in the pit of my stomach, bringing the familiar sensation of golden light with it. My Legacy was tied to my emotions after all. Emotions, instinct…it was all the same in the end. If I lost it, the whole pub might turn into a pile of matchsticks before the minute was up.

"Skye drove him away," Sean went on, totally oblivious to the pressure cooker inside me. "I told him not to marry her. *Cailleach feasa.*"

Understanding flowed through me even though I was useless at learning Gaelic. In all the months I'd been living here, I'd learned a handful of swear words, and that was it even though most of the villagers spoke it fluently.

Cailleach feasa… Sean McKinnon was calling me a witch! And not in a nice way either.

"Boone left because I found out he was a lying scumbag!" I screeched.

The entire pub fell silent, except for the dulcet tones of some traditional Irish music playing on the stereo. A tin whistle trilled, and I almost flung a bolt of magic across the room to shut it up.

"*Ní mórán thú!*" I exclaimed.

"Am not!" Sean shouted at me. "I am not worthless! Take that back!"

"Since when does Skye speak Gaelic?" someone by the fireplace asked.

"Since now, looks like," another man replied.

"Should we get under the table?"

"Wouldn't hurt."

Maggie and Sean stared at me, both their mouths hanging open.

"If you knew half the things I've done… If you

knew…" The talisman hummed against my skin and then flared, scalding my flesh. Slapping a hand over it, I cursed and sank down onto a stool, hiding behind my hair.

"Crow's curse on you," Sean grumbled.

"Shut up, Sean McKinnon!" Maggie exclaimed. "Can't you see Skye's heartbroken?" She rushed around the end of the bar and bent over me. Placing a hand on my back, she rubbed soothing circles. "Do you want to talk about it, Skye?"

I shook my head, brushing my hair away from my face and the tears that had escaped despite the tight hold I'd had on them.

"He wasn't who he said he was," I muttered. "That's all."

"He did show up out of nowhere," Maggie replied. "Never talked about his past. Not even to Aileen."

"But he was good," Sean said. "Everyone knows it."

Maggie clucked her tongue and helped me to my feet. "Drinkin' will do no good for you, Skye Williams. How about you go home, and I'll send over a hot meal for you? I promise I won't get Sean to deliver it."

"No. It's fine," I said. "I've got some work to do at the shop. I'll… I'll be fine."

"Said every woman with a broken heart," I heard her murmur as I walked away.

Another dusting of snow had fallen while I was inside Molly McCreedy's.

Making my way carefully across the icy road, I unlocked the door to Irish Moon and shuffled inside. The crystals hummed merrily as I stood among them, and the talisman around my neck harmonized. I'd almost blown my top at Sean McKinnon and blasted him with my magic. *Go hIfreann leat.*

Rummaging underneath the counter, I took out my tarot cards and began shuffling. If anything were going to show me the way through this pain, it would be the message revealed in the cards. They'd helped me before, so they would again.

Please, not the Chariot, I thought to myself as I drew a card. *Anything but the Chariot.*

Squeezing my eyes shut, I turned over my selection, then took a deep breath. *Now or never…* I opened my eyes and relaxed when I saw the Five of Cups. It was a card of loss, but the loss wasn't total.

Studying the image, I saw that three cups were knocked over, but two were still standing. Holding up the card, I tilted it back and forth, watching the light play on the metallic design. This was one of those 'the cup is half full or half empty' scenarios. I could wallow in my heartbreak, or I could take what I had left and continue to fight.

I didn't want to die, but I didn't want to be alone either.

Getting up off my fat ass, I slunk outside, the cold air burning my cheeks. I glanced up and down the street, studying every facade, picking out all the little details I'd never bothered to notice before.

The Virginia creeper covering Molly McCreedy's had lost all its leaves, leaving behind a mess of vines and woody growths. An old bird's nests lay ruined among the twists, bits of feather blowing in the icy breeze. Mary's Teahouse stood out like a sore thumb, the hot pink neon contrasted to the snow nestled on the ground.

The hawthorn tree had finally lost all its leaves and was full to bursting with little red berries. It was a strange sight to my eyes, only having ever known it in the summer months. It clashed with the teahouse, but it kind of fit into the irreverent spirit of Derrydun.

The lights were on in the window of the handicrafts store, and within, I could see Cheese Wheel Aoife knitting by the fireplace. I wondered if she'd found anything else in Slieveward Bog to go with her ancient cheese.

Glancing up the hill, the ruined tower house was shrouded in mist, the weather really taking a turn for the worse. I couldn't help wondering if it had anything to do with Carman. The last time snow had fallen, she'd snuck back into the country. Was this cold snap a sign Boone had returned to the evil fold?

My headache was stripped raw once more, and I held back a sob. Alone. Was this how Aileen felt all those years ago when she went through her own Crescent Calling? She'd left Dad and me behind and had come home to news her family had been murdered. She'd been alone then, dealing with all this magic brouhaha. How did she handle it? Thinking about Robert O'Keefe, the lawyer who may or may not be a leprechaun, I scoffed. Fat lot of good he was doing. I hadn't seen him since the funeral months and months ago.

Shrinking into my coat, I thought about the people who were here. Humans, innocent and welcoming all the same even though they'd thought Aileen was a little coocoo, and I must be by extension. Maggie cared, and even Sean must, in his own crackpot way. The village was exactly like an extended family that lived in an insane asylum. Everyone was different, but we were all linked despite our abilities and despite me being a witch…and especially despite this being ground zero for a supernatural grudge match.

No matter where I turned, Derrydun was still full of

people who cared about me, and vice versa, no matter what Sean McKinnon dribbled. I had to go on just like Aileen had.

The sound of metal scraping across earth drew my attention to the cottage down the street by the bus stop. Mrs. Boyle was bent over in her garden, shoveling snow from the path, her back all crooked. I didn't want to say she was Derrydun's Boo Radley, but she was the village recluse. An eccentric and borderline-crazy cat lady—without all the cats. The closest I'd seen to a feline army around here was Father O'Donegal's tabby cat shitting in her garden. He got chased with the broom, too.

I'd never stopped to speak to her, mainly because I was terrified of being whacked with her seasonal weapon of choice, and seeing her struggle to tend her garden was really making me feel awful about it. Without Boone here to help her, she was still getting on with it. If old Mrs. Boyle could, then so could I.

Crossing the street, I approached the old woman, taking my life in my hands. I'd seen her chase kids half my age and gain on them, so I knew she had plenty of spritely energy in reserves. Spooking her was the last thing I wanted to do.

"Mrs. Boyle?"

The old woman glanced up at me, her fingers tightening around her shovel. The scowl on her face was positively apocalyptic.

"Can I help you with that?"

She looked me up and down before thrusting the shovel at me. Taking that as a 'hell, yes,' I began scraping the snow from the path, all the way from the gate to her front door. As I worked, she stood and watched me, much like she supervised Boone.

When the last shovelful of snow was cast aside, I wiped the sweat from my forehead and handed back Mrs. Boyle her shovel. Hesitating, I spied movement down the road, and my heart skipped a beat.

A shadow was looming out of the mist, and I froze, watching the misshapen blob grow darker as it approached. When the muffled thumping cleared into definite hoof beats on the asphalt, my heart slowed. It wasn't a fae coming to eat me. It was just old Fergus and his faithful Jack Russell terrier riding on his donkey's back.

Fergus raised his hand as he passed, his dog lifting its head to peer at us. He was going to Molly McCreedy's.

"Do you suppose his donkey gets cold?" I asked the old women as it's hoof beats echoed dully.

Mrs. Boyle scowled at me.

"Do you have any other jobs you need help with?" I added, knowing I wouldn't get any small talk from her that didn't involve foul words in Gaelic.

She shook her head. *"Gread leat."*

It basically meant 'go the hell away,' so I pushed through the gate, making sure I latched it behind me.

Crossing the street, I pressed my nose against the window of the handicraft store. The glass was cold, and my breath began fogging it up. Spying Aoife still by the fireplace, I knocked and waved when she glanced up.

The woman unlocked the door and gestured for me to come in out of the cold. Instantly, the scent of lavender and rose wafted up my nostrils from the display of handmade soaps by the door.

"Skye," she said. "Are you all right, dear? I heard—"

Before she could ask about Boone's disappearance— boy, gossip traveled faster than gastro around here—I picked up a throw rug from the basket by the till. "I was wondering if I could ask you a favor."

"Yes, of course." She eyed the rug in my hands and blinked in bewilderment.

"What do you know about donkey coats?"

CHAPTER 12

"And…we're live."

I peered at the laptop as Mairead clicked a button with a flourish.

"That's it?" I asked. "The website is open for business?"

"Duh." The Goth girl rolled her eyes.

"So how does it work? With the shop and the magical Internet?"

Mairead tapped the updated employee handbook she'd painstakingly worked on since the new computer equipment arrived. "It's all linked, so if someone buys somethin' in the shop, it'll be taken off the website."

"What if someone buys it online?"

"Then the computer won't be able to scan the item if we don't have any others in stock," she said matter-of-factly. "I've put a lot of thought into this, you know."

"I can see the thousand euro I spent on all this hasn't gone to waste," I said, picking up the fancy barcode zapper thingy and brandishing it like a laser pistol. "*Pew! Pew!*"

Mairead snatched the scanner from me and clucked her tongue. "This isn't *Star Wars*."

"Yeah, *Star Wars* is a guaranteed HEA."

"HEA?"

"Happily. Ever. After." I made a face and took out the tarot cards, more out of habit than anything.

"So, when we get new stock, we have to enter it into the computer," she went on. "Then print out barcodes."

"Sounds like a lot of work."

"You'll know how much you have sittin' in the storeroom with a click or two," Mairead complained.

"So the stockroom is all clean and fully itemized?" I raised an eyebrow.

"You don't pay me enough for that."

"I could…" I smiled sweetly and shuffled the tarot cards.

"Is this my shop or yours?"

I shrugged and set the cards on the counter. Fanning them out, I let my palm hover over the top, sensing the energy they were giving off. I hadn't drawn one since I pulled the Five of Cups, and that was a week ago. Things were… Well, they were still raw.

"You're still wearin' the ring," Mairead noted.

I snorted, loving how she called it 'the ring' like it was the One Ring from *Lord of The Rings* and it would eat my soul or something equally as horrifying. *One ring to rule them all…* Anyway, maybe it was hope that made me keep it on. Hope that what Boone and I had was real, and hope that he would come through the door of Irish Moon like nothing had ever changed. Or maybe it was just a reminder of the sacrifices I'd made to ensure the safety of Derrydun, Ireland, and everything else in the world.

Ignoring the tarot cards, I stood and reached for my coat. "Do you think you could hold the fort for a while?"

Mairead narrowed her eyes. "Where are you goin'?"

I knew she partly blamed me for driving Boone away, and so did I, but there was nothing I could do to help that now.

"It's… Witch business," I replied.

"Like that's an excuse," she muttered sullenly.

"It's not an excuse, it's a fact," I declared, shrugging into my trusty leather jacket. "I have to ask a tree a question."

"You're weird."

"I know. Isn't it delightful?"

Outside, the weather was still rotten. Winter seemed to go on forever here, and the dreary sky was a testament to my sour mood. There was nothing to differentiate one day from the next—thick fog blanketed the village and shrouded the tower house every morning, it cleared by mid-morning to gray skies, sometimes we were given the gift of misty rain, and then night fell and brought a frost along with it.

Bundling up in my jacket, I pulled on my old beanie and covered the tips of my ears, and then I shoved my hands into my old faithful fingerless gloves. I hadn't been able to bring myself to wear the ones Boone had given to me at Christmas, so I'd gone back to the ones I'd had before. Old familiars.

The path to the hawthorn was quiet. A little bird flitted through the trees but flew away when it heard me approaching. Everyone had gone and found someplace warm to be, including all the animals. I was the only mad person out here.

Stepping into the clearing, I studied the knotted and

gnarled truck of the ancient hawthorn. It looked different this time of year. Its branches had lost most of their leaves, and thousands of red berries had sprouted in their place. When spring came, I knew it would be white with blossoms, heralding the new season.

Glancing around the clearing, I shivered. Boone and I had shared so many things here. He'd revealed his fox shape to me over there, I'd stabbed his brother in the eye a little to the left, we'd fought the craglorn by that tree stump, and so many other things. Conversations, attempts at unlocking his memories, declarations of love… The list went on.

I couldn't help wondering if I'd managed to crack open the curse on his mind, would things have gone differently between us? If his brother Dub hadn't shown up and lured it out of him, maybe he would still be on my side.

I turned toward the hawthorn and placed my hands on its trunk.

"Did you know who he was?" I asked, tears welling in my eyes. "Did you know he was her son? Did you know he's a thousand-year-old shapeshifter witch?" I may as well have been talking to myself. "You're a useless bunch of biatches, you know that? No wonder everyone hates us."

A hissing and clicking sound echoed behind me, and for a moment, I thought I'd royally peeved off the Crescent ancestors, but I felt darkness looming in the forest. A darkness that was *familiar*.

I jerked around, my eyes widening as I saw a craglorn move through the trees. I hadn't even sensed it coming! There was no excuse. I should've known it was lurking around the village. I was so *stupid*.

Its body was the same bluish black I remembered from the last one I'd faced, and its talons were just as razor sharp, too. Beady, black eyes with no whites stared at me as it froze just inside the clearing. It wasn't as tall or quite as alienesque as its deceased friend, but no less terrifying.

"Magic," it said in a strange, twisted voice. "*Maaagggiiiccc…*"

"I'd turn around, and go back if I were you," I said to the craglorn. "I know you're hungry, but the buffet is closed."

The creature's head tilted to the side, listening intently to what I was saying. "*Magic?*"

I shook my head. "You can't have mine. I need it."

"Hungry…" It glanced at the hawthorn and bared its teeth. "Home. Home. *Home!*"

It leaped forward, jumping on elongated legs, and I almost fell on my ass in fright. I rolled to the side, dodging a swipe of its claws and summoned my magic. I wasn't the same Skye who shat her pants fighting the same creature six, or however long it was, months ago. I didn't need a web to trap it or a charged athame to stab into its leathery hide. All I needed was a can of Crescent whoop ass.

I was strong enough. Just me. Me alone.

My magic rose in an instant, responding to the adrenaline tearing through my veins. The surge of power was a kick in the guts. It was the strongest I'd been yet, and it scared me more than the thought of being gutted by one of those talons.

My golden magic took my breath away as I launched at the craglorn, and the moment the light touched it… Well, a sonic boom had nothing on the way I tore that thing apart.

It wailed, and the sound lodged into my brain. I fell to my knees as the craglorn disintegrated, and the clearing darkened around me.

It'd been so easy to take its life. One second… Something terrible lived inside me. My Legacy wasn't something to be revered. I didn't want it.

"Why did you have to do that?" A tear fell from my eye as I knelt by the scorched earth. "I don't want to kill anything anymore… I don't want to be a Crescent. Not if it's like this. I don't want to care…"

Caring is what makes you different.

My head shot up, and I stared at the hawthorn.

"Who said that?"

Only the wind answered me, fluttering through the trees and rustling the berries on the hawthorn above.

Caring is what made me different? Different from what?

Scurrying forward, I placed my hands on the tree. Closing my eyes, I felt the gnarled bark scratch against my palms as I cast my magic out. Tendrils of golden light probed the hawthorn, but I felt nothing other than the natural growth of the tree. No ancestor spirits, no doorway, and no answers.

Someone had told me about the journey being more important than the destination, but I couldn't remember who. Is that why they wouldn't speak to me?

"No one's going to help me," I said to the tree. "So it looks like I have to help myself."

Wiping away my tears, I brushed off the dirt on my knees and straightened my top. Combing my fingers through my hair, I sucked in a deep breath and centered myself.

I could fight the fae and their mummified craglorn cousins, that much was clear, so casting a few barriers and wards wouldn't harm anyone. It would keep the village and the hawthorns safe or at least slow down anything that decided it wanted to get through badly enough. The magical signature would attract fae like a moth to an open flame, but it didn't seem to matter anymore. Time was running out, and an inbuilt intruder alarm would be more helpful now than before. Boone had warned me against it, but he wasn't here to fly around the village as a gyrfalcon with his gyrfalcon eyes and shapeshifter senses—which I now understood were an added side benefit from his unknown witch abilities—so I had to be proactive on my own.

I couldn't believe it had taken me almost a month to figure this out. *That's what wallowing gets you*, I thought to myself. *A bigger hole to sit your ass in.*

I made my way back to the village with a new purpose. My fingers felt all tingly from my tussle with the craglorn, and I shoved my nausea away. I'd studied barriers and wards in the Crescent spell book and had meditated on the hawthorns more than I probably should have in an attempt to figure out their secrets.

Spotting Fergus's donkey hitched out the front of Molly McCreedy's, I smiled. She was wearing the coat I asked Aoife to make. Emerald green trimmed with earthy brown and lined with the same. It was a sign I was back on the right path, I was sure of it.

Opening the door to Irish Moon, I stepped inside and immediately felt the relieving hum of the crystals. My fingers had just begun getting their feeling back when Mairead blew a raspberry at me.

"Took long enough," she said.

"Just stopping by for some supplies."

"Like what? Fertilizer?"

"Very funny," I shot back at her, picking up a bound wad of sage.

"You better scan that."

"I will."

"What were you doin' out there anyway?"

"I've told you about the hawthorns. I had to see if someone was home," I replied, deciding to omit the part about the craglorn I'd just nuked in the clearing…and the existential crisis I'd had immediately after. "Shit is about to go down."

"Did it tell you that?" Her eyes widened. "I know Carman is comin', but it hasn't seemed real."

"Believe me, I know all about that." I held out the smudge stick for her to scan. "Put me down for four of these."

"What's this for?" she asked, brandishing the scanner.

"I'm making an electric fae fence."

"Are not!"

"Am too!"

The scanner beeped as Mairead tallied up my inventory. I added a bag of pink Himalayan rock salt to the pile and began fiddling with some clear quartz tumbled stones. Maybe I could use these as an anchor to make the spells last longer. There was no way I was walking a thousand miles around the countryside on a weekly basis if I didn't have to. Quartz held a lot of grounding power and would echo the natural energies of the hawthorns. That was if I cast the barrier properly.

"What's the salt for?" Mairead asked, holding up the bag.

"Nothing," I replied. "I like the taste. Goes good on rubbery microwaved vegetables."

She made a face and scanned the barcode as I piled my supplies into a calico bag, which also got zapped with the laser.

"You're goin' now?" Mairead complained as I made for the door.

"I've got no time to waste," I replied, the quartz clacking in the bag. "I'll make it up to you, I promise."

"You better," she grumbled as I left.

Glancing up and down the street, I checked the time on my phone. It was barely lunchtime, so I stopped off at the teahouse to get a sandwich to go. I had a lot of ground to cover before nightfall.

CHAPTER 13

Even in the dead of winter, the forest around Derrydun was brilliant green.

Moss clung to everything—snaking up rocks, clinging to fallen tree trunks, and sprouting wherever there was a dusting of dirt and damp. Pressing my fingers against a patch, it sprang back like a sponge. Lichen clung to the side of the tower house, gray, green, and yellow.

Leaning against the wall, I felt the magic rippling through the ruined structure and stared out over the village. It had been so long since I'd been up here. Maybe once since Boone and I had dug up the athame. Glancing up, I could almost see his ghost perched on the stone above me, looking out for trouble.

Returning my attention to the landscape, I made a mental note of where everything lay. The main street, the lone set of traffic lights, the cottage, the ancient hawthorn, the druid's cave, and the place where Boone said Aileen defeated Hannah the spriggan.

To the right, past the village, was Boone's cottage. I didn't look too far in that direction, the thought of him cozying up to his mother too much to bear. I would be seeing him again that much was certain, but I wasn't sure I would like the way he would look at me when he did.

To the left of my perch were the top fields of Roy's farm, and beyond that, the smudge of smoke gave away the position of his little cottage. Further still was the Ashlyn's property, Maggie's parents, along with their dozen horses.

I'd walked around the lot of it, studying the land, placing quartz, burning sage, and constructing the largest magical barrier Ireland had ever seen. At least, I figured it was. Carman was cursed out of the country, so I assumed she didn't count in my world record attempt. Too bad I couldn't call up Guinness and ask for inclusion in their next annual edition.

I'd found some interesting things, too. The foundations of a long forgotten cottage, another druid cave, a small ring of standing stones, and the edges of a barrow. The dead who lay beneath were long forgotten and hidden from the modern world, but my magic had sensed them through the earth. The dead hawthorn in the glade behind Sean McKinnon's farmhouse was a revelation, but I assumed it had passed long before I came here. Its branches had been gray and brittle, snapping off when I'd curled my hand around a low-lying bough. A doorway lost forever.

When the last quartz crystal had been placed and the spell cast, I'd felt a flare of magic as all the edges joined. Stepping through to the outside, I'd felt coldness that had everything to do with exposure, and when I'd returned within, warmth had spread through my joints, tingling everywhere it went. Even the talisman around my neck heated like it was connected, too.

The barriers had worked but at a cost. In the week after I'd put them up, they'd started going haywire. Everything and anything tripped them, and I was out in the countryside checking every little magical mouse that brushed up against the invisible web. I was all for learning something new every day, but finding out just how many supernatural creatures lived around here through a million false alarms was an annoying lesson for sure.

Now sitting on the hill overlooking Derrydun, I knew the hassle was worth it. The tower house felt like an antenna, the bubble of magic left behind by the witch who had lived here in the seventeen hundreds, Mary Byrne, acting as the magical router in the Wi-Fi network I'd created. I'd totally morphed into Sarah Connor in *Terminator 2: Judgment Day*. In the first movie, she was all girly and whiny, and by the second film, she was a super badass soldier who didn't take any shit lying down. Though the difference in my story was the fact I'd just made Skynet my bitch. Figuratively speaking.

Yesterday, the first craglorn had shown up since the barrier was completed. By the time I'd reached the spot where it had attempted to cross, there was nothing left of it but a pile of ashes. Later that day, the second came along for a stickybeak and got zapped, as well, but by the time the sun rose this morning, they seemed to have learned their lesson. *Don't try to eat the zappy magic.*

I cast out my senses and felt the lingering shadow deep in the forest past the ancient hawthorn. The third craglorn was waiting for a weakness in the barrier to reveal itself or for me to come check on it, it wasn't clear. It paced like a starving lion that scented blood on the air but couldn't get to it.

Still, I couldn't leave it lingering out there. There

would be a whole lot of freaking out and severed limbs if someone stumbled across it, so I followed the path down the hill away from the tower house, my boots crunching on the gravel underfoot. There was another added benefit of my new witch mercenary slash commando job title. I had killer calves, a smaller waistline, and buns of steel.

The forest was becoming familiar now that I'd walked the breadth of it. The rise and fall of the land, the twisting of trees, the fallen foliage, and the rocky landscape were as normal to me as all the buildings and shops in Derrydun. My magic spoke to the land, guiding my way toward the shadow at the border, and it wasn't long before it grew darker. There was a chill in the air that I'd learned was yet another witchy omen, this one a warning.

I saw the craglorn through the trees, so inky blue it was almost black. When it sensed me, it clambered toward the barrier, stopping well short of the zap zone.

Up close, it was hard to believe they were fae before. Ancient, lost, trapped in a world that wasn't their own and cut off from the one thing they needed to survive. *The other realm must be steeped in magic*, I thought. *Absolutely dripping with it. Magic must be their oxygen.*

I wondered what this one was. Was it like the man who'd stolen Alex's face? Or the spriggan who'd tricked Boone and killed my mother? I didn't know how many kinds there were, but I figured there were more than two.

"Who are you?" I asked, no longer afraid of the creature standing two meters away from me.

Eyelids closed over its black eyes before they opened again.

"You've been driven mad by hunger, haven't you?"

It blinked at me again, and I wasn't sure if it even understood what I was saying.

"I don't want to hurt you," I said. "But I will protect myself and those who live in this village. Do you understand?"

It raised its hand, its talons unfurling slowly. Swallowing hard, my gaze locked onto the razor-sharp tips, my stomach churning. Thank goodness it couldn't get through the barrier.

"I…" the craglon rasped. "See… *You…*"

Before I understood what was happening, it stepped toward the barrier and thrust its hand through. The air shimmered and flared gold where its arm touched, and I stumbled back in surprise. It wasn't meant to do that!

I called on my magic and pushed back, forcing the craglorn away. As it pulled its arm back, the barrier flexed and snapped. The shockwave ricocheted through my outstretched arm and blew me off my feet. I landed on my ass, my head spinning and my ears ringing so loudly, I couldn't hear anything else but distortion.

Rubbing my temples, I tried to sit up, but I wasn't sure which way that was. A shadow loomed, and everything in me was screaming danger, but the synapses in my brain were misfiring.

Claws scratched my chest as its hand pushed down onto my stomach, then… I gasped as I felt it sucking greedily at my magic, pulling my Legacy through my skin. It burned, pain blooming through my gut and falling outward. *Oh, cac, this was how it felt?*

I called on my magic, but all it did was make the craglorn drain me faster. The only thing that was left to do was get it off me the old-fashioned way.

I kicked with all my strength…with a little magical oomph to go with it. It cost me, but the craglorn went flying, hitting what was left of the barrier. It fizzed and crackled, zapping the creature, but there wasn't enough juice to turn it into ash.

"I told you," I cried as I dragged myself to my feet, feeling like I had a bad case of indigestion. "I told you I'd protect myself, but you didn't listen."

The craglorn rolled onto its side, hissing and spitting, its back burned from where it had struck the barrier. Blue ooze was weeping through its seared flesh, and I curled my lip.

"I want it back," I exclaimed, advancing on it.

I felt violated in the worst possible way like it had sucked out part of my soul and ate it for brunch.

"*Mmaaggiicc…*" it wailed.

"Mine." I stretched out my arm and called it back, my Legacy flaring through the craglorn's skin as I returned the favor.

I had no idea what I was doing, but something inside me sputtered and flared into life. I pulled my magic back out of that thing, siphoning the golden light it had feasted upon like I was scooping the tasty icing off the top of a slightly moldy donut. How I knew how to do it was beyond me, but I wasn't asking questions.

It writhed on the ground, and I felt a pang of pity for the twisted thing it had become.

"I don't want to do this, you know," I said. "But I have to."

Calling on the entirety of my Legacy, I enveloped the craglorn with golden light, reducing the creature to ash. There was no getting around the fact I had to fight them. None at all.

Glancing at the quartz on the ground, I sighed. *Well, that was a bust.* The barrier was pretty much blown to bits, and all that work I'd done was for nothing. Kneeling by the crystal, I tapped it, hoping there was some charge left. It flared, then died completely. *Nope.* I was learning the hard way why Aileen had never made her own barrier around the village. It didn't work. Not on a scale like this.

Leaving the quartz behind, I made my way back to Derrydun, my mind swirling with the things I'd learned and the failure eating at my conscience. If I could call back my Legacy from a craglorn, could others call theirs back from Carman? Excitement mixed with the throbbing in my ass and stomach, a shred of hope lighting the darkness.

I didn't know what drew me to Molly McCreedy's, but I found myself pushing through the door once I got back to Derrydun. The scent of cooking food, wood smoke, and barley and hops hit my nose, and I breathed deeply, calmed by the familiarity. A group of people sitting by the fireplace turned at my entrance and proceeded to stare. Roy, another farmer and his wife, and Mary Donnelly were huddled together like they were in the midst of a football scrum.

Ever since Boone had left, the gossip mill had been in overdrive. The wheel was spinning faster than the back axle of a car in a *Fast and the Furious* movie, leaving a trail of rubber on the road an inch thick. Glancing down, I saw I was caked with mud, which wasn't helping to slow the constant stream of hearsay.

"She's been wanderin' all over the place burnin' sage," Roy said, his voice floating across the pub. "It's strange, even for her."

"Aileen was always doin' queer things," another farmer added, not caring for his volume.

"Must be a family thing," Mary Donnelly said, eyeing me across the room, sour that her wedding plans had to be thrown out. "They were all like that."

"I can hear you," I practically shouted. "Crazy Skye Williams has nothing wrong with her ears, thank you very much."

"Skye, you're covered in mud," Maggie said, shooing the others away. "What have you been doin' out there?"

If they only knew. Man, that was like my messed-up personal mantra. If only they knew what lengths I was going to protect them from craglorns who hadn't seemed to have forgotten how to use their own magic…even though they were starved and on the road to complete mummification. What a mouthful.

"I slipped," I muttered, eyeing the group in the corner. Old men and gossiping old ladies.

"Did you see the lightnin' before?" Roy asked, ignoring Maggie and me.

"Lightnin'?" the other farmer asked. "There's no lightnin' this time of year."

"Saw it with me own eyes. A bright flare, yellow like a firework."

"You're goin' senile," Mary said. "There's no such thing as yellow lightnin'. Everyone knows it's blue."

"Like the rinse you put in your hair?" Roy shot at her.

Maggie clucked her tongue. "You need a dram of whiskey," she said. "That'll warm you right up. Don't listen to those old eejits."

I sat on a stool, the gravity of what I'd just experienced in the forest, catching up with me. I felt exhaustion tugging on every limb—the physical *and* emotional kind—and watched Maggie fussing behind the bar.

"How are you?" she asked, setting the glass down in front of me.

I knew she was getting at Boone's disappearance, so I shrugged. "As well as I can be, I suppose."

"Aye, it's a difficult thing, to be sure."

"I have…a lot of things going on." I sighed and lifted the glass to my lips. Taking a sip, the liquor burned down my throat and hit my stomach with a bang. Wheezing, I pushed it away as Maggie chuckled.

"Still can't hold your whiskey," she said. "You know if you want to talk about it…"

I nodded. "I know." But I couldn't. Not all of it.

"I'm worried about you, Skye," she murmured, leaning against the bar. "Is somethin' more goin' on?"

I blinked, suddenly on the verge of tears. Over my failed barrier, over sending Boone away, over the fear I felt about Carman's looming assault on the hawthorn, over not being able to tell anyone about it, over protecting Mairead from being dragged back into this whole mess… The list went on, and I hardly had the breath to let it all out. The secret was burning a hole in my heart.

"I think I've just been trying to ignore everything," I said, half lying. "And it's finally catching up with me."

"Ah, we all have to face our hurts at some point," she replied. "That's the law of life. You can't avoid the truth in your heart for long."

"You say that like you've been through it."

"Aye, well most people have their hearts broken at least once in their lifetime," she said with a nod. "But it's what you do next that matters."

My fingers tightened around the glass of whiskey. She was right. How many times did I have to be beaten over the head with it?

"So, what's next, Skye Williams?"

"I'm going to fight," I said, jumping off the stool.

"For?" Maggie called out to me.

"If I told you, I'd have to kill you!"

"That's not reassurin'," she said. "It's slightly terrifyin', is what it is."

A wave of nausea rolled in my stomach, and I tensed.

"Skye?"

"I think I'm going to hurl…"

"Not on the floor! Hold it in! *Hold it in!*" Maggie raced around the end of the bar brandishing a bucket, but…

I doubled over and…

"*Blargh!*"

CHAPTER 14

The moment I got home, I puked neon yellow into the toilet bowl. Again. The color had nothing to do with my magic, by the way. That was when I discovered the mark on my guts.

I stared at the red welt on my stomach in the mirror and grimaced. A handprint with five dots all spaced out to match the five claws the craglorn had pressed against me when it had tried to feed. Gross. The word feed made me want to hurl again.

Opening the cupboard under the sink, I fossicked through the tubes of ointment and soaps Aileen had collected like a pack rat and found a tube of salve that said it worked for bug bites. Cooling burns and insect nibbles. That ought to cover it.

Sitting on the edge of the bath, I rubbed it into the… What should I call it? A suck mark? I shivered and made a face. Whatever it was, it was a close call. The closest I'd had since that swarm of sluagh tried to drown me at Croagh Patrick.

I seriously felt like imploding. I couldn't do this

anymore! I was the last of the most badass coven to have ever lived? Yeah, right! I couldn't even stop a craglorn from sucking my magic let alone keep a magical barrier in working order. I was supposed to be able to do the impossible, right? *Ugh.*

The sound of furious knocking at the front door broke through my inner tantrum, and my heart skipped a dozen beats. Dropping the tube of ointment, it landed on the floor with a plop.

"I'm so over this!" I shrieked, barreling out of the bathroom and down the stairs. "I'll kick your ass, then I'll fry you to a crisp! *Just you wait!*"

Wrenching open the front door, I froze, not expecting what was standing on the stoop. A woman was waiting patiently, and when she saw me, her face lit up.

Her hair was long, black and streaked with silver, her face was wrinkled with age, her clothes were rumpled and caked with dirt... She looked like an older version of me. Either I was in a time warp and had come back to visit myself or... *Aileen.* It couldn't be her because she'd been drowned in the earth by a spriggan, which meant a fae had taken her form to trick me. A fae brought here by the barrier, which was no longer working thanks to that hungry craglorn.

For a split second, I was dazed, but my instincts kicked in, and it was on like Donkey Kong.

I raised my hands and forced my magic to flare around my fingers. The moment it shot out toward her, the woman returned fire. Her magic collided with mine, gold and bright. I stumbled back a step as I realized this wasn't a trick. No one had stolen her face.

It was Aileen.

"*Mum?*" I whispered, my hands falling to my side.

She smiled as our magic faded from the air, her eyes crinkling at the corners.

"Skye," she said. "I come back to you now at the turnin' of the tide."

I frowned. "Wait. Isn't that a line from *Lord of the Rings*?"

"Yes, but it's a good one. Very fittin', don't you think?"

I was flabbergasted, and my mouth flapped uselessly. "What… How… When…"

"Can I come inside? It's rather chilly out here."

I stood aside as she came in, the reality of her being alive not hitting me as hard as it should have. Not yet, anyway. I was sure I would be visiting the toilet bowl again soon.

The moment the door closed, Aileen pulled me into a tight hug, squashing the air out of my lungs. "My daughter," she murmured. "Why do you smell like midge cream?"

I didn't know what to say, so I blurted the first thing that came to mind. "Aileen… Carman's here. She's in Ireland."

She pulled away, staring at me with unguarded concern. "How?"

"Aileen…" My bottom lip trembled, and suddenly, I was two years old again with a scraped knee. "I stuffed everything up."

"I seriously doubt that. You're my daughter." She glanced over my shoulder and frowned. "Why is there a dead tree in my living room?"

I'd totally forgotten about the Christmas tree that had turned brown a week ago. "I think you'll find the cottage is legally mine."

"Hmm. You're right..." Aileen wrapped her arm around my waist and led me into the lounge room.

"Are you hungry? You must be." Wriggling out of her grasp, I legged it into the kitchen.

Leaning against the counter, I drew in a breath, my lungs burning. Aileen was alive. Aileen was alive and in the next room. *My mother*. I'd hated her for leaving for so long but had then come to understand her and the Crescent Calling—maybe I even loved her a little—and now she'd come back to life. She better not be a zombie because I was fresh out of brains.

Reaching for the last packet of chocolate biscuits, I went back into the lounge room and set them on the coffee table.

"*Oohh*, Chocolate Kimberleys," Aileen exclaimed, opening the packet.

"How are you here?" I asked. "I mean... I've seen a lot of weird shit but resurrection? This is a new bag of crazy."

"I never made it to the ancestors," she replied, nibbling on a chocolate biscuit. "I was in between, and it took me a while to find my way back. I didn't expect it, to be honest. When I told Boone to protect you, I thought I was a goner." She humphed. "Luckily, I didn't arrive because they're the most difficult bunch of spirits I've ever dealt with. I wasn't ready for an eternity with them. It would drive me around the bend and back."

I screwed my face up, wondering why that sounded so familiar. "I think I was there."

Aileen almost dropped her biscuit. "What? On the other side?"

"In the hawthorn, you mean? That's where they are, right?"

Aileen nodded.

"Uh… There was a thing with a craglorn and…" I didn't want to say Boone's name because then I would have to explain, and I was humiliated enough with all my stabbing in the dark and nonsense dreams.

"And?" she prodded.

I lifted up my T-shirt, stopping an inch away from flashing her.

"Skye!" Her hand flew to her mouth.

"This was another one," I said lamely. "Today. I put midge cream on it. It seems to be helping."

"There was another one?"

"Three, if you want to get specific. Wait. Five. Yeah, there were five."

"*Skye Williams*," Aileen exclaimed, getting all motherly.

"Am I grounded?"

"I think we're past that stage, don't you? How much did it take?"

"Not much."

She eyed me for a moment, then seemed satisfied. This day was getting more whacked as it went.

"*Ahh*, it's good to be home…" Shoving the last of the biscuit into her mouth, Aileen kicked up her feet and began picking leaves and grit from her hair. "Tell me about the craglorn. Do you feel sick?"

"I barfed big time, but I was able to get it back."

"What? The vomit? Skye, that's disgustin'."

"No! I don't lick up neon yellow spew, thank you very much. I'm talking about my magic. You know, the Crescent Legacy or whatever fancy-pants name you want to slap on it. I took it back, then zapped its ass. *Pow!*" I swatted the air with my fist.

"You took it back?" Aileen stopped playing with her hair.

I nodded and poked at the mark on my stomach. "Served it right. I warned it, but it didn't listen. It was all *mmaaggiiccc, blergh!*"

Aileen looked thoughtful but didn't share any of it with me. Maybe I wasn't supposed to take my magic back. Is that what made me throw up? Better not have because there went my plan for getting stolen Legacies back to their rightful owners. Throwing up was the worst.

My stomach flip-flopped again. This was happening way too fast. Thinking about the Chariot, I wondered if this was what it heralded all along. It wouldn't be the first time I'd misinterpreted the tarot cards. Aileen was back... Like, *really* back.

"Are you really here?" I wanted to pinch Aileen to make sure she was solid. I'd seen some crazy things since moving to Derrydun, but this was the craziest by far. "I mean, I've had weird dreams about purple typewriters, and there was this thing about elephant toast, and there was this fae that stole the face of my ex-boyfriend, and I poked a wolf's eye out with a stick... Oh! And there was the swim I took with the sluagh, and the hawthorn tried to warn me about the Nightshade Witches, then there—"

"Skye," Aileen interrupted. "Calm down. I'm really here."

"How? I mean, you just said you never made it to the other side, but how?"

She sank back into the armchair and drew in a deep breath before letting it out in one big whoosh.

"I was pulled into the earth," she began. "But my magic cocooned me."

"But we went to the clearing," I argued. "There was nothing there. Nothing at all. The earth wasn't disturbed or anything. I don't understand..."

"After survivin' this long, I've stopped askin' questions myself. Though I gathered it mustn't have been my time."

"But you must remember something," I argued. "That can't be it!"

"I remember usin' the last of me strength to cast a cocoon around myself. Then there was darkness. Lots of darkness. I suppose that's when I died, and you were Called. Somethin' brought me back and stopped me from crossin' into the hawthorn with the ancestors, but I can't really explain what. Perhaps me spell spared me and gave me another chance. It felt like I went for a really long swim through sludge, not knowin' which way I was supposed to go. Then I swam into the forest, pulled myself out of the ground, and here we are. I'm glad you've got biscuits."

"Well, I'm glad you're here," I said sullenly. "I've got a lot of mess to clean up. I could do with a hand."

"I can't fix this for you, Skye. I'm not a plot device dropped in at the right moment to make all your mistakes go away. I'm not in control of the coven anymore."

"Why not?"

"Technically, I did die but not really. It messed up the bloodline, and magic can be very literal about these things."

"So this is some kind of magical time warp where the space-time continuum has folded in on itself?"

Aileen blinked, looking bewildered, then shrugged. "You could say it like that, but the simple version is the mantle passed to you, and once you've got it, you can't hand it back. You're in charge of the coven now, and whatever comes next, you must lead with your Legacy."

"So, I'm your boss."

"Kind of."

"You sort of died, and even though you're back, you got demoted anyway?"

"I wouldn't say it like that," she said with a huff.

"It's exactly like that."

"Where's Boone?" Aileen asked, abruptly changing the subject. She looked around the cottage as if he would poke his head out from behind the couch at any second.

"Uh…"

"Skye?"

I played with the ring on my finger and looked anywhere but at Aileen. The floral curtains had a rather interesting pattern to them even though they were ugly as sin, and I'd been too lazy to change them over.

"Skye?" Aileen prodded again. "Where is Boone?"

"Gone," I replied with a sigh.

"Gone? Where?"

"Home." It was as simple as that.

Aileen's gaze dropped to my finger, and her eyebrows knitted together. "His memory came back."

It was a statement, not a question, so I didn't bother replying.

"Where is home, Skye?"

"Carman," I replied, twisting the ring around my finger. "He's one of Carman's sons."

Aileen let her head fall. "And that ring?"

"I love him," I whispered, the words tearing open the wound in my heart again. "He asked me to marry him at Christmas and…"

"Oh, Skye…"

"I've got a lot to tell you," I murmured. "So much has happened."

"Then you better start at the beginnin'."

"But we don't have time," I complained. "Carman is

coming, and she could be here at any moment! I've been trying to prepare, but…" I felt like bursting into tears. "I told you. I stuffed everything up."

"We have time," Aileen said, placing her hand on my knee. "This is important, Skye. Take a deep breath, and tell me about arrivin' in Derrydun. Did Robert O'Keefe help you?"

Doing as she said, I breathed deeply, then exclaimed, "Let me tell you about that scoundrel, Robert O'Keefe!"

CHAPTER 15

When the sun rose the next morning, it broke through the clouds for the first time in months.

I scarcely had the brainpower to work out the omen to go with it. I'd had an hour of sleep on the back of an entire night bringing Aileen up to speed on everything that had happened since she'd, well, carked it. The craglorns, the ritual, what I'd done to the Nightshade Witches, the visions the hawthorn had shown me, the athame I'd found buried in the tower house, the swim I'd taken with the sluagh, Boone's wolf shape and the healing powers of his animal tongue…all of it. Well, except the part where Boone and I'd done it in a ditch. I left that bit out. There were some things you just didn't tell your mother.

I was currently sitting at the kitchen table in a state of fatigue and shock, a can of energy drink open in front of me. Aileen—all washed and smelling like roses—was sorting through the fridge, clucking her tongue at every over-processed, genetically modified convenient food item I'd stuffed in there. I was having another nonsense dream. If that were the case, then who knew what it would manifest as when I woke up. Arctic, honeysuckle, powder puff, ice cream most likely.

"I've been having dreams," I said.

"Of?"

I shrugged.

"I can't hear you shruggin'," Aileen declared, her head still stuffed into the fridge.

"I don't know," I said. "That's the point. I mean, I know I've been dreaming something important, but when I try to recall them, it's all purple monkey, elephant, toaster, lima bean."

"Lima bean?"

"I made that last one up."

"Hmm…" she mused, stacking up the dozen frozen meals on top of the frozen pizza. "It could mean a lot of things."

"Like?"

"You say the hawthorn's been talkin' to you?"

I nodded.

She looked at me curiously, then shrugged. "We'll just have to wait and see."

"Is that it?" I exclaimed. "We just have to wait and see? What if I have a brain tumor?"

"You don't have a brain tumor," she retorted. "I would've smelled it."

"That's not weird at all!"

The resemblance was uncanny. Aileen even thought the same way I did—in sarcasm and pop culture references. Was sass a genetic trait? I was fast becoming a believer.

"What's normal in our world, Skye? We talk to magical trees and protect humanity from starvin' creatures trapped here from another plane of existence. Leprechauns are real, shadow people are real, and golden light shoots from our fingertips!"

My shoulders sank. "Point."

Our world was crazy and wonderful, but it had a darker side. One that had been with us for a thousand years.

After hoping the hawthorn had been right about Aileen being alive and finding nothing at the site of her death, after all the disappointments—I couldn't quite fathom the fact she was pulling out all my frozen meals from the freezer and scolding me like I was five years old. Seeing my mother in the kitchen, checking how well I adulted, was really messing with my head. I never had any of this growing up, and I'd come to accept she was gone forever only a few months ago.

I wondered what Dad would think about all this. Did he know about her being a witch? I didn't think so. It wasn't like I was accidentally going to set something on fire in the midst of a tantrum. My magic had been bound long before Aileen had answered the Crescent Calling. It wasn't until Robert O'Keefe had shown up and unbound my Legacy with his golden pen that things had started getting weird.

That was another revelation from last night. Robert O'Keefe, the Danny DeVito lookalike, was a leprechaun. It explained a lot.

"Mum… Aileen… I mean…"

She glanced up from the fridge and frowned. "Call me what you like, Skye. I know I wasn't there. I don't blame you. You can call me 'that bitch-faced scrag' if you like, and I won't ground you or anythin'."

"It's just…" I didn't know how to express what I was thinking without hurting her feelings. "I get it now, but when you left, it took me a while to understand you weren't coming back. I got used to it then. Lots of kids I went to school with had single parents, so I didn't think I was special or anything. When Robert O'Keefe showed up… It hadn't been long since Dad passed away and…"

"I regret what happened with your father, I do… I wanted to protect you from all of this. Both of you." She picked up a frozen chicken meal and scowled at it. "I never told him about this life. He never knew what I could do, and back then… I didn't want you to be drawn into this awful existence. Once, I imagine it would've been wonderful bein' a witch."

"Yeah, a thousand years ago," I drawled.

"Exactly. It's always been a burden I wanted to spare you from. Look at that mark on your stomach. I never wanted you to face a craglorn let alone have your magic siphoned by one."

"Yeah, you wanted to spare me until Boone got you killed." I knew it wasn't his fault, but I was in a mood, and my mouth was running away with itself. *What a bitch.*

Aileen shook her head. "No, it wasn't his fault. It was what it was and nothin' more. I assume he told you about it?"

I nodded, knowing I was just sulking and making excuses. Sometimes, shit just happened, and there was nothing anyone could do about it. Unless it was me and my quick temper, shit had nothing to do with it.

"He wasn't going to tell me," I said. "About his memories being unlocked."

"Boone's brother came to Derrydun because Carman wanted to separate you," Aileen said matter-of-factly. "Together, you were stronger."

"And I sent him straight back to her," I muttered. "If

I'd just spoken rationally to him, then he'd be here right now."

"Maybe, maybe not. It's no use dwellin' on what-ifs, Skye."

"That's easy for you to say!" I threw my hands into the air in frustration.

"Why would you think that?" she asked. "You're lucky. Your grandmother, great-aunt, and great-grandmother didn't come back. I knew of my magic, but I was never any good at it. I was the only child, the last Crescent in a new generation, *much like you*, and I was hopeless. Magic never came easy to me, not like everyone else. I'd watch them all twirl around the hawthorn, flick their fingers and make the clearin' bloom. When I tried, I made everythin' wither and die. Always too much magic, my mother would tell me. *You're not tryin'*. I wanted to be anywhere else but here. Guardin' a tree when I could be backpackin' across Europe and bein' promiscuous? That was much more excitin'.'"

"So when you came back…"

"I was takin' a stab in the dark. I knew all the pieces—in that, our stories differ—but controllin' what I'd spent a lifetime rebellin' against wasn't easy."

I opened my mouth to say 'you didn't have Carman breathing down your neck,' but it was just another excuse. I'd been full of them since she'd turned up last night. Coming back from the dead was a huge thing, and here I was just waiting to dump all my crap on her head. I finally had a mother, but it didn't mean I had to regress twenty years into adolescence. Besides, she said it herself. I was the head of the coven now. I guess that meant I had to act like I knew what I was doing at least some of the time.

I sighed and rubbed my finger over the condensation on the side of the pizza box.

"The worst was knowin' I wasn't there when they needed me most," she added. "Guilt held me back for a long time."

What did I say to that? The Nightshade Witches had burned our family alive while she was living in Australia and raising a family. Who knew what would've happened if she'd remained. Aileen was right about all the what-ifs. All we had was now.

"We can't afford to wait anymore," Aileen said. "Now I'm back, it's only a matter of time before Carman finds out. We have the element of surprise."

She was right. If Carman knew Aileen was here, she would alter her plans to compensate, and we would lose the only advantage we had.

"Right, down to business then?" I asked.

"I'd love to have more time with you, but magical apocalypses and all."

"Maybe after, we could…" I shrugged.

"We're goin' to kick her witch ass," Aileen declared. "But we have to have a plan."

"Any ideas? Because that stabbing in the dark thing…"

"We need to lure her here."

"*What?*" I shot to my feet, the chair almost falling over. "You do know if she gets to the hawthorn, it's game over. Kaput." I dragged my finger across my neck. "*Curtains for the Crescents!*"

"We can't leave Derrydun, Skye. Without anyone guardin' the hawthorn, everyone will be in danger."

"What's stopping her from breaking into any of the hundreds of hawthorn trees over Ireland, anyway?"

"They're all sealed."

"I know that but why ours? It's where the spell was cast, wasn't it?"

Aileen nodded. "Crescent spell, Crescent hawthorn. We've got the master key flowin' in our veins. The network has to originate from somewhere, and it's that tree out in the forest."

"Then we have to lure Carman here and not fail. Easy...*not.*"

I had no idea how we were going to do that. I hoped Aileen had some aces up her sleeve because my suggestion was to troll Carman on Facebook. Somehow, I didn't think the thousand-year-old witch had a profile.

"If we take out Carman, the rest will fall," she added.

My mouth dropped open. "So the fae who follow her, her sons, her power..."

"It's all linked to her."

"That makes things a little easier."

"She'll be heavily guarded...and warded, so no. Not so easy."

"And Boone?"

Aileen ignored me, which signaled the answer wasn't a good one, crossed the kitchen and peered out the window. "We have another problem to deal with first."

"We have more problems?" I wailed.

"I can't go out there," she stated, pointing to the outside world. "They'll think I'm a zombie."

"You'll have to come out of the closet eventually," I said. "You can't hide in here the rest of your life. I should call Mairead."

"Mairead? What about Mairead?"

"Uh..." I'd left that part out, too, about the kidnapping and the disclosure.

"*Skye...*"

"I, uh... There was an incident with a talisman and a van with tinted windows, a kidnapping, and Mairead dropped out of Trinity. Then there was a thing with her managing Irish Moon and wanting to be an artist. Oh! And her parents disowned her, so she lived with me for a while, then they made up, and she put barcodes on all the stuff in the shop, and here we are." I picked up the frozen pizza. "Hungry?"

"*Skye!*" Aileen exclaimed. "*In all my life...*"

I winced. "Am I grounded?"

CHAPTER 16

I raced out of the cottage, acting a sight more spritely than I was feeling. I was running on fumes, fueled by adrenaline, powered by life or death. I leaped over the garden bed, commando rolled over the low stone fence, fell on my ass, and then catapulted toward the main street like I was competing in the Olympics.

Rounding the corner, I weaved around a startled Father O'Donegal, who shook his fist at me as I went, hurdled over a pile of donkey poop, then landed on the doormat in front of Irish Moon like a long jumper landing in a sandpit. New world record! Someone play the national anthem!

"*Mairead!*" I shrieked, barging into the shop.

"Give it a rest," the Goth girl grumbled, emerging from underneath the counter.

"What are you doing under there?"

"I'm hungover."

Skipping the lecture on the dangers of binge drinking and brain cells, I grasped her shoulders and shook. Her head flopped back and forth, and her scowl deepened.

"What part of *hungover* didn't you understand?" she declared, swatting my hands away.

"I've got news!" I chortled. "Big news! Humungous, ginormous, elephant-sized news!" I flung my arms wide.

"Are you on drugs?"

"Am I…" I pouted and turned my face to the side. "Why, I never!"

She rolled her eyes and blew a strand of hair off her face. "All right, all right, spit it out."

"Close the shop, and go to the cottage," I said. "There's a surprise waiting for you there."

"A surprise?"

"Don't get too excited. There's a lot to do!"

"A lot of what?" Mairead's frown deepened. "Better not be work."

"It's time," I said mysteriously.

"Time?" Her expression began to change as understanding dawned. "You mean?"

"*Yep.*" I nodded. "We've got a plan, but it's going to take everything we've got."

"What plan? Who's we?"

I snatched a calico bag off the shelf and began tipping crystals into it. Points, tumbled stones, agate slices, geodes. You name it, it went in.

"Hey! I've got to scan those!" Mairead exclaimed squirming. "You'll ruin the system!"

"Here," I said, thrusting the heavy bag at her. "Take these to the cottage. Aileen will explain the rest."

"Aileen? But… Skye, are you sure you're not…"

"I'm not high!" I exclaimed. "Go, Mairead. We haven't got much time to prepare. We're going to lure that bitch Carman here and end her for good."

"But—"

"Go!" I thrust my finger toward the door.

"What about—"

"Mairead!"

"Fine!" She rushed out of the shop and disappeared.

That girl was about to get the shock of her life. *Hmm…
I should've packed a defibrillator.*

Taking her lead, I followed her outside, though I
had another errand to run before I could make it back
home to help Aileen with the crystals. Locking the
door behind me, I sprinted across the street to the
teahouse.

Mary Donnelly was the biggest gossip in Derrydun. If
there were such a thing as an emergency phone tree in this
place, she would be right at the top like a star on a
Christmas tree. One word from her and the whole village
would mobilize.

"Good mornin', Skye," the little old lady said as I
barged in. "What's ticklin' your nether regions this
mornin'?"

When she held up a bucket, I grimaced.

"That was one time!" I exclaimed.

"Can't take any chances, dear," she replied. "My back
isn't what it used to be."

Taking it from her, I hugged the plastic against my
chest, more to appease her than to catch any wayward
spew. It was slightly humiliating, but not as awkward as
things were going to get.

"I'm calling the banners," I declared.

"The what?" She blinked at me, the reference going
straight over her head.

"It's a *Game of Thrones* reference."

"A Game of who?"

"A Game of…" I clucked my tongue. "I'll lend you the

boxed set. Right now, I'm calling a village meeting. Tell everyone."

"A village meetin'? The last time we had one of those was when…" She trailed off, looking troubled.

"When my family was burned alive?" I raised an eyebrow.

"Why, I wasn't goin' to say it so bluntly," Mary said with a huff.

"Can you do it?"

"Call the banners?" Mary asked with a quizzical look. "What's so important? You've been actin' really strange lately."

"No, I haven't!"

"Well, ever since Boone—"

"I'm going to stop you right there," I declared holding out my hand. "This is very important. The life or death kind. It involves the whole village, so if you'll humor me, pick up the phone and start ding-a-linging."

Mary tilted her head to the side and clucked her tongue. Picking up a pair of tongs, she lifted the glass lid off the cookie display and retrieved a double chocolate chip, slipped it into a paper bag, and thrust it at me.

"Eat up, dear. A little sugar will have you feelin' better in no time."

I wasn't about to argue over a free chocolate cookie, so I took the bag and pointed to the phone. "Remember. Life or death."

I didn't look back as I ran from the shop, darted across the road without looking, and crossed the garden out the front of the cottage. I was hardly feeling the cold anymore, and the added sunshine warmed my back and shoulders as I raced across the village.

The talisman factory was in full swing by the time I barged into the lounge room.

The first and second steps in our 'make it up as we went along' plan were in action, but if no one turned up at Molly McCreedy's tonight, I wasn't sure what we would do. The flare our magic was sending up while we charged all these crystals was epic. It was a giant neon sign in the shape of a middle finger Crescent salute aimed right at Carman, and the first piece of bait on the lure. Yet more evidence my barrier had been a pathetic fart in the wind.

Aileen and Mairead were sitting on the floor when I walked in, and there was a mountain of crystals piled on the coffee table.

"I'm still worried she's goin' to eat my brains," the Goth girl said, glancing up from her notebook. She'd been scrawling down barcode numbers so she could update the computer later. Talk about obsessive.

"Unless you're a lamb, I wouldn't worry about it," Aileen quipped, closing her fingers around a little spike of clear quartz.

"*Gross.*"

"I'm glad to see you too, Mairead."

A smile crept across Mairead's black lipstick-stained lips. "Me, too."

"How did it go with Mary?" Aileen asked me.

"She gave me a cookie and sent me on my way, is what she did," I complained, sitting on the floor.

"She would've picked up the phone the moment you left," Aileen replied. "Mary Donnelly is a busybody who lives for scandal. Don't let her blue rinse fool you."

"So we can count on the whole village being there tonight?"

Mairead blew a raspberry and rolled her eyes. "*Duh.* Nothin' else happens around here."

"But a magical cataclysm?" I raised my eyebrows as I reached for a crystal, adding my magic to the mix. "How can we ask them to fight with us?"

"Don't underestimate the Irish," Aileen declared.

"If only we had a few more athames." I glanced at the dagger on the coffee table, studying the silver and gold hilt. Crescent moons wove an intricate pattern, signifying that it was a Crescent Witch heirloom. It had worked wonders on that craglorn. Stick it in and *poof!*

Wow. That didn't sound dirty at all.

"We're doin' what we can," Aileen said. "Anythin' more would be too much risk to our Legacy. We need our strength."

"When do you think she'll come?" Mairead asked.

"It's difficult to say. Tomorrow, the day after, next week… She might call our bluff, and all this would've been for nothin'."

"Will Boone be with her?"

"Err…" I glanced at my mother, my stomach becoming unsettled for the millionth time in the last day.

Aileen nodded. "Most likely."

"But you said…" the girl started to wail.

"I know what I said. Skye's go it covered." She glanced at me pointedly.

Aileen hadn't said it in as many words, but if Boone was linked to Carman and she fell, then he would go down with her. Unless I did something to get him back.

"Yeah," I said, focusing on the crystal in my palm. "Covered from head to foot." *Liar.*

Aileen threaded her fingers through Fergus's donkey's mane and sighed.

She was right about Mary Donnelly. From the mass of people chattering inside, the Derrydun phone tree worked a treat. Gossip really was the currency of getting people together in this town. Unless the gossip was about me, then it was another story. Curiosity had won out yet again!

"This shouldn't be hard at all," Aileen said, showing the first sliver of uneasiness she'd felt since coming back from the dead. Or clawing her way out of the earth, or whatever it was she'd done.

"It's weird more than anything," I quipped, holding the bag of talismans against my stomach, which was still tender despite the midge cream. "Are you ready for the collective gasp?"

"Oh, let's get it over with." Aileen strode forward and wrenched the door open, leaving me to scramble behind her. "Rip it off like a sticky plaster."

"What's a sticky plaster?" I called out after her, but it wasn't really the time to question the cultural differences of what was obviously another name for a Band-Aid.

The moment we stepped into the pub, all eyes turned toward us, and there was a simultaneous intake of air. It was so silent I could've heard Fergus's notorious 'silent and deadly' farts Maggie always complained about. Then a glass smashed on the floor.

"*Ó mo dhia!*" someone exclaimed.

"It's a ghost!" someone else shouted.

"What the *cac* is goin' on?" Roy demanded.

"Surprise!" I said lamely.

"There's a gas leak," Aoife said, pressing her palm against her forehead. "We're all high as kites."

"So… One, we're witches," I said, holding up a finger.

"Two, we need your help with this one little thing…" I held up another finger, promptly turning red when I realized I was flipping off the entire pub. "Three, Aileen has resurrected herself!"

"As you can see, I'm very much alive," Aileen said, addressing the assembled villagers. "I had an unfortunate tussle with a spriggan who drowned me in the earth, but I found my way back. It was all quite unexpected."

"A twiggan?" Roy asked, his brow furrowing.

"*Spriggan*," she corrected. "A fae whose true form is a tree."

"You expect us to believe you were attacked by a tree?" Sean exclaimed,

"Oh, shut your pie hole," Aileen said, glaring at him. "I see you haven't changed."

"Twiggan," I said with a giggle. "I'll have to remember that one."

"I always said you were a witch," Sean McKinnon declared. "Felt it in me bones."

"The only thing you've ever felt in your bones is the stench of whiskey," Maggie said clipping him around the ear. "Don't be an eejit."

"If they say they're witches, they ought to prove it," he went on, rubbing the side of his head.

He had a point, but there was a glaring indicator standing right next to me, too.

"Is it safe?" I asked Aileen, uneasy about using my magic away from the hawthorn even though there was one outside in spitting distance. Not to mention our production line that afternoon. What if it didn't gel with the plan?

"That's convenient," Sean exclaimed. "When it comes to the crunch—"

"Aileen has come back from the dead," Mary Donnelly

said, cutting him off with a stern glare. "I think that's proof enough."

"She could've faked it," he muttered.

"Where's Boone?" someone asked.

"Yeah," Sean added. "Where is he, Skye?"

"He went back to where he came from," I replied. "He's with his mother."

Heads turned and started to murmur among themselves.

"His mother?" Roy asked. "He never talked about any mother afore."

I glanced at Aileen, who smiled before turning toward the villagers. "When Bone came to us, he'd lost his memory," she explained. "I found him in the forest and took him in."

"He had amnesia?" Sean asked, scratching his head. "But…"

"Boone is like us," I said. "Like me and Aileen but much more."

"Boone is a witch?" Maggie asked. "Are you sure?"

"Boone is a shapeshifter," Aileen went on. "When I found him, he'd been in the shape of a gyrfalcon, but his main shape is a fox. Lately, he's been able to shift into a wolf."

Roy's mouth fell open. "That fox!" he exclaimed, banging his fist on the table. "There was a fox runnin' around the top fields when he went missin' that time. You're sayin' that was him?"

I nodded. "Yep."

"I'll tan his backside!" the farmer yelled, his face reddening.

"This is all very outlandish," Mary said. "What's this have to do with anythin'?"

I turned to Aileen. "Shall you do the honors, or shall I?"

"You're the head of the Crescents," my mother replied. "This is your story now."

"That's a total cop-out," I complained. "I hate public speaking."

"So do I," she quipped, sitting beside Aoife, who promptly pinched her.

Typical.

Taking a deep breath, I began. *"Once upon a time..."*

I told them about the Crescent Witches and how they'd sealed the way between Ireland and the fae realm a thousand years before. I told them about Carman's lust for power and what would happen to the world if she opened the way. I told them the story of the Nightshade Witches and how they conspired to kill the family I'd never had the chance to know, how Lucy had deceived and kidnapped me, and I told of their punishment. I told them everything I knew about Boone's predicament, his brothers, and his true parentage. I told them about the true power of the hawthorns and the spirits who lived inside them. And I told them about the craglorn and the fae that'd stolen Alex's face.

I told them everything, leaving nothing out. Well, except for the naughty bits.

Finally, I explained what we needed to do to save magic and Ireland from the power Carman wanted to unleash.

I was well aware everyone was staring at me with their mouths hanging open, half in a state of disbelief and the other in shock. The whole thing was outlandish and dramatic, much like a supernatural soap opera. Asking them to believe and then fight beside a couple of smart-mouthed witches was probably a step too far, but we'd run out of options.

"This won't be easy," I said. "And I can't promise that no one will get hurt, but we'll do our best to protect you all from Carman and whatever she brings with her."

"*Boone*," Sean muttered, loud enough for me to hear and loud enough to snap the villagers out of their stupor.

The room erupted into a deafening hubbub, insults flying around like monkeys in a zoo flinging poo at each other.

I was contemplating flipping a table on its side and hiding behind it when Mrs. Boyle slammed the end of her shovel against the floor. The metal sent a *boom* through the room, silencing everyone. We turned to stare as the tight-lipped old woman stood and assumed a pose that looked like she was channeling Gandalf in his 'you shall not pass' stance from the *Lord of The Rings* movies. I'd only ever heard her shout Irish swear words, so whatever she was about to say had to be good.

We all stared at her, holding our breath, waiting for her pearl of wisdom. Then…

"*You have my broom.*"

I made a face and glanced around the room. Broom? Like she was swearing her sword to us? I didn't even know if that was a thing without a round table and a castle. Or a fellowship en route to Mt. Doom.

"I think that means she's cool with all this," Mairead said, breaking the confused silence.

Heads began to nod, and one by one, others began to stand.

"Blasphemy!" Father O'Donegal shouted. "This is blasphemy of the highest order!"

"Oh, shut your pie hole, Finnegan," little Mary Donnelly declared.

"Your name is Finnegan O'Donegal?" I exclaimed. "Anyway, remember that time at my mother's funeral when your cat sat on the altar and licked its balls?"

"He let his cat lick his balls at my funeral?" Aileen exclaimed.

"Blasphemy!" Mairead called out from the peanut gallery.

"Sit down, Finnegan," Roy said, shoving the old minister down into his seat. "Let's hear what these girls have to say. If some witch hell-bent on destroyin' Derrydun is on her way, then I want to know about it. I had enough trouble with that fox!"

"You believe us?" I asked. "You really believe us?"

"Unless this is some kind of mass delusion, and Aileen isn't really standing there, then I'd say we believe you," Mark Ashlyn said.

"It sure explains a lot," Maggie added, smiling at her dad. "All these years we thought you were just weird."

"They are weird," Mairead called out.

"I thought the devil lived inside them," Grace, Mairead's mother, stated.

"Weird but worth fightin' for," Roy declared. "What's the plan?"

Reaching for the calico bag full of crystals, I said, "We've made talismans to protect you. They're not foolproof, but they're the best we've got."

Mairead took the bag from me and helped hand them around. Mary Donnelly gasped as her crystal flared, shining a golden light through her fingers.

"*Mo dhia,*" she whispered.

"Father O'Donegal," I said, holding out a crystal. "Will you take one?"

He scowled, then glanced around at the other villagers. "The Bible teaches tolerance," he said after a moment. "Also forgiveness, love, and understandin'."

I grasped his hand and placed the piece of glowing yellow quartz into his palm. "Then we're on the same page."

He nodded. "Aye."

Standing, I moved toward the bar where Aileen had retreated to. She was sipping a glass of whiskey, and I wrinkled my nose. I was sure I would never get used to the stuff. Maybe that was the Australian coming out in me. I'd gladly have a beer instead.

"What now?" I asked, watching the villagers compare crystals. All in all, they'd taken the whole 'Derrydun was about to become a magical battleground' thing pretty well.

"We watch," Aileen replied. "And we wait. Carman will come soon enough, and when she does..."

"*We'll be ready.*"

CHAPTER 17

It felt like summer.

The sun was warming my shoulders, and I shivered as a bead of sweat trickled down my spine. My black hair was twisted into a loose braid that I'd pulled forward so the breeze could cool the back of my neck. My toes dug into the earth, rocks and leaf litter scratching the soles of my bare feet.

Glancing up, I saw the hawthorn towering above me, its branches laden with tiny white blossoms. The barest hint of green shimmered through the petals, rendering depth to the scene.

I stepped forward, knowing this was a dream…or a vision sent to me from the ancestor spirits. There was no way I could tell the difference. Besides, after this long enduring the latest episode in the Crescent TV series, I kind of just went with it.

Glancing over my shoulder, I checked to make sure I hadn't been followed. The forest was silent, and the village beyond hadn't even noticed I'd skipped out on the Beltane festival early. Good, that meant I had time.

The door was back, the cast iron dark against the trunk of the hawthorn. I was going through again, that much was obvious, but why? Was this a premonition or a glimpse of the past? My thoughts didn't seem to be my own, yet…

Everything inside me was screaming to not open the door as my hand reached out. Don't open the door! My fingers curled around the latch. *Open the door, Skye.*

I twisted, the latch unhooked, and I pulled…

White light streamed through the opening, and I stepped through, the sun blinding. Raising my arm, I covered my eyes and breathed in the perfumed air.

"I was hoping you'd come," a voice said.

"Don't open the door!" I shouted.

I sat bolt upright, my chest heaving and my thoughts all fuzzy. I was back in my bedroom, the first rays of dawn clawing at the sky.

"Skye?"

I glanced down at Aileen, who'd been asleep next to me. She was wide awake now, pushing to her elbows and frowning at me like I'd sprouted a second head during the night.

Rubbing my eyes, I attempted to recall the dream. It was clearer this time, the nonsense only misting half of what I'd seen.

"I had another dream," I murmured, picking the grit off my eyelashes.

"Of?"

"The hawthorn… And…" I gasped as I realized what I'd seen. "The doorway. I went through…"

Aileen was in full sit-up mode by this stage.

Beltane, bare feet, blossoms on the hawthorn. They were all things I'd never seen or done. I didn't recognize the voice, either. *I was hoping you'd come.* It was very male, but it wasn't Boone.

"What did you see?"

"Nothing, I…" I blinked, but I was pretty sure that was the moment I woke up. It was always the way with dreams. The money shot was always left out, like humanity's curse was to always be left wanting more. Except for sex dreams, but that was another story I didn't want to discuss with my mother.

"It was me, but it wasn't," I went on. "Like I was living another life, but it was still like I am now. But not…" I frowned, my shoulders sinking. "Does that make any sense."

"A little."

"Then why am I dreaming this? It can't just be a psychological thing, right? My subconscious could be manifesting the things I'm worried about… That's a way stress can manifest…"

"You don't need a therapist, Skye," Aileen said. "I think someone's with you."

"What?" I immediately grabbed my boobs and tried to hide them even though she was the only one looking at me. Someone was… All those showers and naked posing in the mirror and…*ohhhh* sex with Boone. O. M. *G!* "Are you serious? Who?"

"A Crescent," she replied, laughing at my reaction.

"An ancestor?" I rolled my eyes. "Now they want to help. *Typical.* It's kind of pervy."

"They are sticklers for showin' up on their own terms."

I flopped back into bed and buried underneath the covers. If Aileen were right, then how long had this spirit been piggybacking my life? It was super creepy, but it explained a lot of things. The nonsense dreams for one, and the random voices I'd been hearing. Oh! And my magic had been flaring up more than usual. I'd assumed it was just growing pains, but it could totally be some wayward spirit short-circuiting my magical motherboard.

Flinging the blankets off me, I sat up again. "I could speak Gaelic!" I declared. "When I got angry with Sean after Boone left, I ranted at him in Gaelic! The only word I know how to say is shit."

Aileen scratched her head. "Everyone always learns the curse words first."

"Why?" I asked the dark room more than my mother. "What do you want from me?"

"Skye," Aileen said, placing her hand on my arm. "We don't know if someone's there. Not for sure."

"Then how do we find out?"

She sighed and glanced out the bedroom window. From the look on her face, I wasn't sure she knew. I'd hoped Aileen was a know-it-all witchy almanac when she'd shown up, but her knowledge was limited. Not as much as mine, but she'd been in the same position as I had once. A lifetime of study and still the entire power of the Crescent Legacy was beyond her. So much had been lost in the wake of Carman, I couldn't fathom it.

Finally, she said, "Let's take a walk."

"But it's too early," I complained. "Five more minutes!"

"Bein' early won't hurt our plans," she said, whacking me on the shoulder.

I dragged myself out of bed and moaned as my feet hit the cold floor. There was definitely a freaky spirit tagging along because I hated feet and that included mine.

"I call the shower first!" I shouted, darting out of the bedroom and down the hall.

Closing myself in the bathroom, I flipped on the light and stared at my reflection.

"Hello," I whispered. "Who might you be?"

And in true Crescent ancestor spirit, nothing answered me. Nothing at all.

Carman would arrive any day now.

Outside, the air was still, crisp, and full of anticipation. The calm before the storm. It was the ultimate cliché, but it was true. The whole village was jumping from foot to foot like they all had the runs, and I was feeling pretty much the same. It was so bad that the Topaz was out of toilet paper.

Instead of going straight up the hill to the tower house, Aileen and I detoured via the main street. The lights were on in the teahouse, casting a warm glow out into the misty dawn. We could see Mary Donnelly within, stocking up the sandwich counter with ingredients. She'd already topped up the muffins and cookies, and my mouth began to water. *Double chocolate chip!* The village would be well fed this week, that was for sure.

I turned at the sound of hooves clomping on asphalt and saw Fergus and his entourage emerging from the ghostly tendrils of fog that clung to the landscape.

"Good mornin', Fergus," Aileen said, holding the calico bag she'd brought along with us against her chest.

Stopping beside the donkey, I scratched behind her ears as the Jack Russell stood and wagged his tail. The little dog had a crystal attached to his collar, and the donkey had one stitched into the lining of her coat. It wasn't until last night at the village meeting I'd finally learned they were named the very obvious Jack and Donkey.

After we'd revealed the truth about the Crescents, we'd given everyone a crash course in spotting fae and craglorns. Without inherited magic to guide them, having talismans would make it a great deal easier. While acting as a layer of protection, the crystals would also react to any supernatural juju by warming, so not only were they useful in our quest to protect Derrydun but they were also handy on a cold day.

"Mornin'," Fergus rasped, burying into his coat.

"Anythin' out there?"

"Quiet," he replied, glancing at me. "More than usual."

"Thanks, Fergus," I said, rubbing Jack on the head.

More than usual. They were on their way then.

"We appreciate your help," Aileen added.

We'd arranged the village to be on the lookout for Carman's coming, and they were out in shifts, patrolling the forest and the roads. A lot of people were still skeptical of our story, but I was kind of glad about that. Blind acceptance wasn't the greatest thing even though it would've been easier. Free will, free thought, and earned trust were more valuable prizes.

We let Fergus go on his way and walked toward the traffic lights before turning north and climbing upward past the limit of Roy's farm. The fields were empty. The flock had been herded into the sheds by his cottage further to the west.

"Aileen?"

"Hmm?"

"You know how I was able to take back my magic from the craglorn?" I said as we climbed the hill. "If there's any chance of capturing Carman, then I could help give the witches back their stolen Legacies."

"Perhaps, but it might not work out that way."

She didn't have to say it. We might have to kill her to stop her from opening the doorway. *Take her out, and the rest will fall.* It was the surest way to end this war before it got any worse. Still, I didn't like knowing all those witches would have lost their magic forever.

"And Boone?" I asked. "If Carman dies, he'll die, too?"

Aileen nodded.

I let my head fall into my hands and swallowed a sob. My knees wobbled beneath me, and it was all I could do not to fall into a heap. So much had happened in the last few days, and after so long waiting… It was all too much. The thought of losing Boone forever was like taking a hot poker to my heart.

"Do you want to save him?"

"I love him, " I whispered. "Even after all of this…" I toyed with the ring on my finger, twisting it around and around.

"There's good in him, Skye," my mother reassured me. "Even with his amnesia, it wouldn't have been enough to stop his true nature from shinin' through."

"But I thought his wolf form was his true nature?"

"It's what he is," she explained. "Not who. If Boone were evil, then his story here in Derrydun would've been as different as night and day."

"You're saying…"

"I don't believe he came here out of spite or because it was some kind of plot."

"Then why?"

"Because it was his destiny."

Destiny… It was such a strange word. To think

everything we were doing had already played out on some mystical level was infuriating, yet calming at the same time. I wasn't sure I would ever fully understand this life. Why magic was the way it was, how we could exist, and what the point of it all was, but maybe that was it. We weren't supposed to know everything. No one should wield absolute power. No one at all.

I scoffed at the irony and wiped my tears. It was the journey that mattered, not the destination. Boone was right. He always was, after all, and so was Aileen. I saw it now as clear as the Legacy flowing through my veins.

"Then we have to convince him to come home before Carman dies," I said, my hopes rising. "Because Derrydun is his real home."

"Sever her link to him…"

"And he'll be free to live or die as he chooses."

The tower house loomed above us, and I stared up at its ruined walls, a chill spreading through my bones. It was about to become the central computer in another kind of magical network, not unlike Skynet from the *Terminator* movies.

It felt like I'd come full circle. From the first time I'd faced a craglorn with Boone to the eve of the ultimate battle. This time, the tactics were similar but on a grander scale. By recycling the crystals I'd used in my failed barrier, we could create the largest web Ireland had ever seen. It would trap Carman inside—along with the ancient hawthorn and the whole of Derrydun—and then we would skewer her. There were more moving parts than that, but it was the 'too long, didn't read' version. Trap. Skewer. *Bam!*

If it didn't work, plan B was to improvise.

I opened the metal door that closed off the ruin from

wandering tourists and allowed Aileen to enter first. Following her into the darkness, we re-emerged into what would've once been the main hall. It was open to the sky and the weather, and I squirmed as I watched my mother walk the perimeter of the room. Finally, she stopped in the center.

Taking the large chunk of clear quartz out of her bag, she placed it on the ground and turned it around until she was satisfied with the placement.

"Can we resell that?" I asked, studying the spiked facets of the crystal. It was one of the largest geodes in Irish Moon and was worth almost four hundred euros.

"After a cleansin', yes."

"Good. I've been trying to improve the shop's bottom line." I blew out a long breath. "So we aren't actually activating the spell yet?"

"It'll lay dormant until we need it," Aileen replied. "It should be undetectable on this kind of scale."

"*Should* be?"

She shrugged and rose to her feet, her eyes misting with tears.

"I'm not that insolent, am I?" I made a face. "It is a four-hundred-euro chunk of crystal we're just leaving out here. The word should at a time like this—"

"You're everythin' I ever imagined," Aileen declared, wiping away her own tears.

"*Errr...*" I squirmed, not liking the attention. I could never take a compliment without wondering when the punch line was coming.

"I thought of you every day," she went on. "Wonderin' what you'd be like, if you were as feisty as me or calm like your father."

"Aileen..."

"You're the one, Skye," she declared, grasping my shoulders. "After a thousand years, you're the one who'll lead us all into a new age."

"You're really freaking me out," I muttered. "Do we have to do this? I'm not a savior."

"Skye, you need to hear this." Her expression turned serious as she stared at me. "When the time comes, open yourself."

"Open myself?"

"When it happens, you'll know."

"That's not weird at all," I said, making a face.

I wasn't a fabled chosen one. I was just Skye, the reluctant witch with a flair for the dramatic. I would do what had to be done, and that was all. There was nothing prophetic about it at all. The stars definitely did not align on the day of my birth, I could vouch for that.

"Come." Aileen smiled and shook her head, gesturing for me to step toward the center of the ruin.

Kneeling beside the crystal, we clasped hands and rested our free hands on the quartz, making a circle.

"For the witches of Ireland," I whispered.

"Today, we are one coven," Aileen added.

"*Forever, we are one.*"

CHAPTER 18

Standing underneath the branches of the hawthorn in the middle of the main road through Derrydun, I sighed.

I hated waiting. Especially when it was all world hanging in the balance and shite.

"It's getting colder," Maggie said, her breath vaporizing on the air. "Are you sure it's not just a freak weather event?"

"This is how Carman got into Ireland," I said, shaking my head. "Under the cover of snow."

Roy paced behind us, clutching a shotgun, Mairead was lingering under the eave of Molly McCreedy's, Mary Donnelly was handing out cookies, and Mrs. Boyle was standing guard over her garden, shovel in hand.

The rest of the villagers were spread out, manning the perimeter and waiting for signs of Carman's approach. Aileen was holed up in the teahouse, out of sight—in the only warm place in town—and out of mind.

"It won't be long now," I murmured, glancing at the sky.

"*Hooo!*"

"What's that?" Mairead called out. "Is it an owl?"

"I don't think so," Mary said, dusting off her empty tray. "Owls only come out at night."

We all turned our attention up the road to the single set of traffic lights.

"*Hooo!*"

"There it is again," Roy said.

"What do you suppose it is?" Maggie asked.

"*Hooo!*" Sean McKinnon appeared around the corner, sprinting down the road and waving his arms like a madman.

"It's Sean," Mairead said. "I've never heard him make that sound before."

"Is his ass on fire?" Maggie asked. "I've never seen him run so fast."

"*The snakes are comin'!*" he bellowed. "*The snakes are comin'!*"

"Snakes?" I glanced at Aileen, who'd emerged from the teahouse.

"There are no snakes in Ireland," she said with a *humph*. "Is he drunk?"

Sean came to a stop in front of our group and doubled over, trying to catch his breath. "I'm." *Puff.* "Not." *Puff.* "Shittin'." *Puff.* "Around."

"Not a drop of whiskey in him," Maggie said, sniffing the air around the Irishman. "Just the stench of not showerin' for a few days."

"I showered this mornin' and washed meself with Imperial Leather soap, I'll be thankin' you very much."

"Must be the Brut deodorant then," Aileen said.

"Aileen!" Sean complained. "Skye, you believe me, right?"

"Where'd you see them?" I asked, in a mood to believe everything on the eve—or day—of battle.

"Comin' down the road past the Ashlyn's," he replied. "A whole swarm of 'em. Brown ones, green ones, black ones, stripy ones. Mean lookin' sons of—"

"Then they're here," I murmured, glancing at Aileen again. "Finally."

"Boone'll be with them," she said, grasping my hands. "Are you ready to face him?"

I nodded. I'd fretted enough over his true nature. There was nothing left to do now but fight.

"It's Carman," I said. "All of it. Take out her, and the rest will fall. I must have a chance to win him back before…"

Aileen nodded. "I'll do what I can."

"We'll do what we can," Maggie said.

"Me, too," Sean added.

Roy nodded gruffly and lifted his shotgun.

"Spread the word," I said to Mairead. "This is not a drill."

"On it," the Goth girl declared and ran off to warn the others.

"Aileen, go back inside. I've got this."

A mass of writhing darkness appeared on the horizon and powered toward us, slithering down the road in one great heap.

"*Ó mo dhia!*" Mary exclaimed.

"What do we do?" Sean asked.

Say a prayer…

I steeled myself as the mass bore down on us, and I held out my hands, hoping for the best.

Mary clutched her crystal as the snakes wove around her and the other villagers, the talismans protecting them from being overwhelmed. Mrs. Boyle screeched something in Gaelic and chopped off the head of a snake with her shovel, then turned to slice and dice another.

I clutched my own talisman and felt out my Legacy. A rush of magic flowed from my core, and I pushed it outward.

"Go away," I whispered. "No snakes allowed!"

I forced my magic outward, letting my instincts guide me. The barrier around me grew and grew until it exploded outward, sending snakes flying through the air.

"*Argh!*" Maggie shrieked. "There's one in me hair! Get it out! *Get it out!*"

She jumped from foot to foot as Roy picked the little snake from her curly locks and flung it down for Mrs. Boyle to sever in half.

The snakes hissed and struck out, and I shoved them away with my magic, the closest to the blast exploding. Little bits of snake guts flew everywhere, and Mary Donnelly shrieked.

"This wasn't in the plan!" she exclaimed.

As the rest of the snakes slithered away, I glanced back up the road. The traffic lights blinked on and off a few times, then died completely. Overhead, the sky darkened, the clouds brimming with darkness.

"I don't like this," Sean said, clutching Maggie's arm.

"You're supposed to protect me," she complained.

"If I protect you, will you give me a kiss?"

"Eww! No!"

"*Shh,*" I hissed holding up my hand.

Silence fell behind me as I stared into the distance. I could feel something coming. Power crackled, charging the air, and I knew. This was it.

I saw the wolves first—three massive silver beasts

prowling through the mist, their eyes catching the light and shining ominously. Behind them was a woman, her footfalls silent. I wasn't sure what I was expecting, but it wasn't this. Maybe a parade with a float and confetti and a marching band. Or a chariot made out of the bones of her victims drawn by a hellhound.

No, Carman just wandered into Derrydun on her own two feet, escorted by her three sons in their wolf shapes. It was a little anticlimactic.

When she saw us waiting for her in front of the hawthorn, she moved ahead, taking the lead. She was exactly how I remembered her from the vision she'd dragged me into. Willowy, freckled, wild auburn hair, and beautiful beyond compare. Though it was tainted with a spiteful streak that made her eyes shine like ice.

She'd donned modern clothing, leaving the flowy dress at home. Boots, leather pants, black T-shirt, and a matching leather jacket. Total dominatrix style. All that was missing was the whip, but odds were, she had a magical one she planned to spank me with.

The three wolves prowled behind her, their heads lowered and their teeth bared. The one in front was huge, its fur tinged copper around its head and tail. The second was more silver but had a puckered hole on the left side of its face. That one was rub-a-dub one-eyed Dub. Trailing behind was the third and most silver of the trio. *Boone.*

My heart leaped into my throat as the entourage of doom approached. I didn't need to cast out my magic to sense the link between Carman and her sons. The thread that wound around Boone was the brightest of them all. It flared in my mind's eye like a red corruption, stoking the fire that fueled my anger. *He didn't have a choice anymore.* Not unless he was strong enough to break free.

The wolves began to shift, their bones snapping and their bodies taking back the fur as their human skin emerged. When they stood, the three brothers were completely butt naked, and each was as hot as the other. Black hair, smoldering eyes—eye in Dub's case—six-packs and tight ass cheeks.

"Boone!" Sean McKinnon wailed as he saw his friend standing on the wrong side of the divide.

"He's naked!" Mary Donnelly shrieked, covering her eyes.

"Wow," Maggie breathed, tilting her head to the side. "What a sna—"

"*Shhh!*" Mairead slapped her on the arm, then sneaked another peek. "Wow, you're right. That's a huge—"

"Enough!" I said. "Boone's got a big ding-dong, so what. He's still connected to her. I can feel it…"

"Connected?" Sean McKinnon asked. "You mean she's controllin' him?"

I nodded. "Stand behind me and stick to the plan, okay? No sudden movements. That means you, Sean."

They nodded, clutching their weapons of choice as I peeled away from them and went to meet my arch nemesis.

"Finally," Carman said, standing a good ten meters away from the little group of villagers at my back and me. "Now we meet face-to-face, Skye Williams."

"Still a raging ginger minge, I see," I drawled. "Without the help of a vision to Photoshop out those fine lines, you're a real mess. You really show your thousand years up close." It was a total lie, Carman was perfection, but anything that peeved her off was satisfying right now.

Her eyes narrowed, but it was the only indicator she gave that my words hit home. *I would take it.*

"You're only delaying the inevitable," Carman said,

raking her cold gaze over me. "I will have what I came for."

"Nah ah!" I said, wiggling my finger at her. "Sorry to burst your world domination bubble, but I don't think so. You've been voted off the island, so it's time to go!"

"Aren't her demands adorable, boys? What do you say Dother?"

Dub and Dother chuckled, but Boone didn't move at all. Carman either had a strong hold over him, or he hated me so much he couldn't bring himself to react.

"One, you'll relinquish control over Boone," I said, ticking my demands off on my fingers. "Two, you can leave peacefully, or three, we can do this the hard way."

Carman's lips curved, then she burst out into laughter, glancing at her sons. "Did you hear that? She wants your little brother."

"My schlong is bigger than his," Dub said.

"You want to measure?" the other brother asked.

Boone narrowed his eyes and brooded.

"Even with one eye, I can still see your dick is shriveling in the cold, Dother," Dub said with a growl.

Ignoring the sibling rivalry, I sought out Boone's gaze. If I couldn't convince him to come home and come back to me, then we risked losing him forever. I couldn't go on without him. I wanted to spend eternity at his side, annoying the *cac* out of him and forcing him to watch all eight seasons of *Game of Thrones* with me over and over until he'd learned all the lines. Then we would continue with *Buffy the Vampire Slayer* and do all that stuff with Mary Donnelly's spring wedding.

I felt the ring on my finger and twisted the band around and around.

"Boone… I was wrong," I said, my heartbeat speeding up to impossible levels. "I should've listened to you. I shouldn't have reacted like I did. I should've fought for you."

"What?" he scoffed. "No but?"

"No but." I shook my head, ignoring the smug look on Carman's face. "I want you to come home. We all do. I *will* fight for you."

"Home?" Carman declared. "This place? *Please.*"

"I'm not talking to you!" I shouted, my magic flaring. "I'm talking to *Boone.*"

"You tell her, Skye!" Mairead shouted.

"Give that bitch what for!" Maggie added.

"All I see before me is a pathetic mess. A witch who doesn't know up from down and twenty humans." The witch laughed and shook out her hair. "You have no power here, Skye Williams, *last* Crescent Witch."

"Maybe not," I said, glancing at Boone. "But I have love and family."

"I have my sons and all the power of Ireland behind me," Carman shouted. "You have nothing! Stand aside or be annihilated. It's your choice. Do you want your human friends to die?"

Empty bravado. I felt the thread connecting Boone to his mother and silently willed him to sever it. My gaze met his, and I mouthed the words, *I love you.* At that moment, I swore his eyes widened slightly, but I couldn't be sure. He was still entwined with Carman, and we were out of time.

"The only person who's dying today is you," I said, my lip curling. "This is where it ends." Turning to Boone, I cast out my magic and caught his. *Whatever happens next… know that I will always love you.*

I raised my hand, hoping he would see the ring was still where he'd placed it, and to signal our trump card. Carman's gaze flickered to the side as Aileen emerged from Mary's Teahouse and came to join me.

The ancient witch's expression fell, and she let out an unearthly scream that vibrated through my bones. "*Noooo!*"

Turning, I reached out for Aileen's hand. "*Now!*"

Our Legacy flared in a whoosh of wind, blowing our hair upward. The sky erupted overhead, a thread of golden light shooting out of the tower house. The tendril snaked across the clouds, separating into dozens of spidery beams as the central crystal connected with the outer boundary. The web flared brightly as it was completed, and then it faded, the afterimage burned into my retina.

"Kill them!" Carman wailed. "Kill them all!"

"She's a bit dramatic," Aileen said, tilting her head to the side.

"I guess it's time to fight for real this time," I replied.

My mother smiled. "Go get him."

Carman flung her hands out at us with a cry, and shadows erupted around her and flew toward us with terrifying speed.

"Sluagh!" I cried, covering my face with my arms.

"Get down!" Aileen shouted.

The sluagh weaved right around me, buffeting my body with a *whoosh* of violent wind. They weren't aiming for me, they were going for the humans!

"*The crystals!*" I exclaimed as the shadows sped toward the villagers.

Roy immediately dropped his shotgun and fumbled in his pocket. He fell onto his ass as he thrust the piece of quartz into the air just as a sluagh bore down onto his position. A flare of golden light met the creature, and it wailed, altering its path and zooming toward the sky. Up and up it went before it slammed into the web and literally went *poof.*

The other villagers did the same, standing shoulder to shoulder in a long line, brandishing their crystals. Aileen ran to help them as I turned my focus to Carman and the wolves. I had to separate Boone from his brothers, sever his link to Carman, and kill her. Easy...*not.*

The three men shifted once more, their bodies exploding into their wolf forms. It wasn't anything like I'd seen Boone do before, not until the night of the ritual. There was no other way to describe it. They'd seemed to have turned inside out. *That had to hurt.*

They edged toward me, teeth bared and dripping saliva as sluagh exploded overhead like fireworks. One snap from one set of those jaws and I was a goner. Totally kaput. I raised my hand and called on my magic, hoping the spirit that had latched onto me wouldn't fudge with me now.

Please, don't overload, I pleaded. *Not now. Please, not now.*

I let the athame slip down my other sleeve. Curling my hand around the hilt, I held the blade steady, eyeing the two wolves as they prowled toward me. If they were hoping for an easy fight, they had another thing coming. This knife was more than sharp enough for three.

"Boone..." I murmured. "Please, don't make me do this... *Please...*"

Dother snapped his jaws and leaped, but a ball of silver fur collided with him, knocking him to the side. They rolled over and over as I swiped the athame at Dub's eye.

"I told you I'd poke the other one out if you ever came back!" I shrieked. "Come a little closer. Here *puppy, puppy, puppy!*"

Dub's haunches tensed, and he launched himself into the air with a growl, his jaws opening. *Ó mo dhia!*

Silver collided with him, too, the streak so fast it caught me off guard. Boone! *He was fighting back!*

"Stop it!" Carman exclaimed, jabbing a finger in my direction. "Kill her! *Kill the Crescent!*"

Dub and Dain snapped and snarled, fighting one another while Dother lay motionless on the side of the road, his coat stained red.

Boone's jaws crunched down on Dub's neck, and I winced, brandishing the athame. Finally, wolf-Boone glanced up and focused on Carman, his lips curling back to show his stained teeth.

"My children!" she shrieked, holding her palms toward Boone. "My boys! My precious boys!"

He began to change, his bones snapping, and his paws twisting. He howled in pain, writhing on the ground.

"Stop it!" I shrieked at her. "*Stop it!*"

Carman wasn't listening, her face was contorted, malice dripping from her twisted smile. This was her idea of punishment? *Bitch!*

Boone's human form cowered on the road, the fur that had been matted with his brother's blood now stuck to his skin. He forced himself to his knees even though he was shaking uncontrollably.

"You had no power over me then, and you have none over me now!" he shouted. "*Get outta me head!*"

Carman took a step toward him, her boot treading in Dother's blood. "You're grounded, Dain. You thought your last punishment was bad. The curse I'll put on you will torment you for *eternity*."

"Great parenting skills," I muttered. "And I thought I was unqualified."

Boone rose to his feet, the blood of his brothers caked onto his skin. The air began to crackle around him, and I knew. He was breaking the chains that bound him to his mother. He was coming home. *He was coming back to me.*

He fell to his knees with a cry, his chest heaving, and the tether broke, forcing Carman to recoil.

"No!" She lurched forward, raising her hands and casting the curse she'd threatened him with. Golden light streamed from her fingers, rushing toward Boone, who was lying helpless on the ground, his eyes sad and accepting.

No!

I wasn't prepared for the color of her Legacy, but I was quick enough to leap between them and deflect the curse before it hit him, or me for that matter. It shot off into the sky, flaring as it dissolved against the web covering Derrydun.

"Stay away from him." I stood between them, giving Carman a look that was designed to wither.

"Skye…" Boone moaned, and I felt his hand curl around my ankle.

I tensed but didn't look back. "I told you," I murmured. "I'm going to fight for you."

I felt a rush as he poured his Legacy into my body. It joined with mine, bright and clear, as Carman bore down on me.

Aileen was right, I mused. *We are stronger together.*

"Let's see if she's still the coward I remember," Carman said, grabbing my arm. "It's time to face me…*sister*."

"Huh?" The air was forced from my lungs as I was torn away from Boone and the rest of reality.

Summer was back.

The sun shone, and golden light streamed through the

green canopy of the forest. The woody scent of the earth filled my nostrils as I breathed deep. I would give Carman a point for this one. Her visions were super realistic.

I had bare feet again. Always with the feet. Feet were the grossest thing ever. Toe jam, warts, crusty heel skin. *Ugh, I wanted to vomit.*

"Look at me."

I turned at the sound of Carman's voice, and our eyes met. She looked younger, more innocent, her cheeks and nose dusted with freckles. Her red hair was loose and wild, the simple linen shift she wore looking like it was from a different era. Behind her, the ancient hawthorn stood tall, but not as tall as it did now. Was this what the clearing looked like a thousand years ago? Everything was so…*different.*

"Siobhan," Carman said. "Stop hiding behind the baby. Come forth."

"I'm not a baby!" I exclaimed. "I don't know who this Siobhan is!"

"Siobhan is my *sister*," she said with a hiss. "The matriarch of the Crescent Witches, and the bitch who forced me out of my home. My own sister!"

She slapped my cheek, forcing my head to the side. My face stung, but I barely felt it. Carman was a Crescent Witch? *Holy guacamole!*

"So this is about revenge," I murmured. "You want to destroy the world for what? A little tiff with your sister? A thousand-year-old grudge for this…" I shook my head.

Carman waved her hand through the air, and the vision shimmered.

"They killed him," she said, her eyes filling with tears. "The fae took him from me, and what did the Crescents do? Nothing. Look at him, Siobhan. *Look at him!*"

"Look at who?"

"*My husband!*"

She forced me to look at the charred and bloody remains of what was once Boone's father. Twisted, torn, unrecognizable.

"I'm not Siobhan," I said. "I'm Skye."

"She's there," Carman said, shaking me. "Why do you think I needed you to break the curse? Her blood runs in your veins, you naive child. You are Siobhan! Her spirit is so tightly coiled around yours it's a wonder you don't choke on her self-righteousness."

The dreams, the flare-ups in my magic, the ritual, the voices… Aileen was right. Someone was piggybacking on me. If I was a descendant of Siobhan, that also meant that I was related to Carman. *Errmm…great.* I was pretty sure that meant I'd been about to marry my cousin, and it was even more direct now that I had ancient witch blood.

"I'm here, sister," I heard myself say.

"*Finally.*"

"This is folly," Siobhan murmured. "All this death, sister, and for what end? Revenge is an empty cause."

"You sealed the doorways. You forced millions into starvation. You trapped our parents on the other side!" Carman scoffed and shook her head in disbelief. "And you stand there and judge me! They murdered Finn!"

"You conspired to steal the power of the fae realm for your own gain. You corrupted your children and forced them into slavery. You were caught and given a choice, sister. Death or exile. Were we wrong to offer it to you?"

"Your mistake was my gain," she said with a smirk. "You tarnished the Crescent Legacy for all time while giving me the opportunity to rise again."

"Both worlds would have perished," Siobhan said, her temper never once rising. "Your actions ignited a war."

"They started it!" Carman shrieked. "They started it by killing my husband. My one true love. You know all about that... *fae-lover*."

"I lost a love that day, too, sister." Siobhan's voice cracked, and I felt the wave of despair hit the ancestor who'd melded her spirit with mine. The dreams... Siobhan was going through the door to meet her secret lover! Talk about a soap opera. "We all made sacrifices for the greater good."

Carman's face twisted, her cheeks stained with tears. She was heartbroken, the pain of her husband's death had twisted her into something dark. Her thirst for revenge wouldn't be complete until both realms were a smoking ruin. The people who took her husband, and the people who denied her revenge. Carman was a world-killer.

"Justify what you did all you like," she snarled. "There's nothing you can do to stop me now. I would give my life to see Finn avenged."

"Sister, *please*..."

"It's over, Siobhan. Get used to utter desolation."

**

My head ached something fierce, not to mention I stung all over.

The backs of my arms were bleeding, and the knees of my jeans were ripped to shreds. Where was I?

Blinking, it took a minute for my vision to clear. Above, I could see familiar snarled branches and red berries. Thousands and thousands of red berries. *Cac!* I'd been dragged to the ancient hawthorn, which meant...

"I've won," Carman said to no one in particular. "After all this time, I've finally won."

"No..." I moaned, rolling onto my side. Where was everyone? Where was Boone?

A clunk and a creak echoing across the clearing forced my head to rise, then I turned my face away as white light streamed from the base of the hawthorn. A burst of magic flowed over me, pure and intoxicating. Power like that couldn't come from Carman. It had to be...

The doorway was open!

The light was blinding, and I raised my hand to shield my eyes from the glare. Was this it? Was this how the apocalypse began?

"Skye! *Get out of the way!*"

The sound of Aileen's voice tore me out of my stupor, and I twisted, rocks digging into my back as I commando rolled my ass out of the line of fire. *They were here!*

A silent shockwave exploded from somewhere in front of me, and the trees around the clearing shuddered violently.

Hands grasped me under the arms, and I was dragged away from the hawthorn. I kicked and cried out, reaching for the light and where Carman had been. I couldn't see her, the light from the fae realm far too bright. Had she already crossed?

The athame... *Where was the athame?*

"*Shh,*" a familiar voice crooned.

Warm eyes met mine, and I crumpled against a familiar strong chest. Someone had given him a shirt. It wasn't black and red checks, but it covered all his indecent parts.

"Boone?" I whispered.

He smiled. "I've got you."

"But..."

He glanced up, his body radiating with a power I'd never felt before. *His true form…*

"It's not over yet," he said. "Can you stand?"

I nodded, my fingers finding the curve of his jaw. "Let's finish this."

CHAPTER 19

People were running past us as Boone helped me to my feet.

Sean McKinnon, Roy, Maggie, Mairead, Mary Donnelly, Fergus and his furry companions, Mark and Fiona Ashlyn, Mairead's parents—Beth and Gregory, Cheese Wheel Aoife, Father O'Donegal, even Mrs. Boyle. They all rushed through the forest and into the clearing and formed a circle around Carman, who was pinned to the ground by a burst of golden light.

Aileen.

She stood above the ancient witch, her hand outstretched and her silver-streaked hair flowing backward. Behind them, the base of the hawthorn was alight with a blinding glow.

Aileen was the only thing standing in the way of Carman crossing over, but something amazing was happening. The villagers formed a circle around Carman, their arms linked at the elbows and their crystals clutched in their hands. Even Donkey had joined the chain, Fergus and Mary grasping her mane. Jack stood on his best mate's back, his teeth bared, and the little spear of quartz on his collar glowed a bright shade of yellow.

I ached all over. I could feel my joints grinding together and the cuts on my knees and arms stinging as I moved toward the circle. Boone's arm slid from my waist, and his hand grasped mine as I wound my other with Aileen's hand. Sean yanked Boone into the circle with a grin, happy to have his best friend back and mostly in one piece.

The entire village of Derrydun surrounded Carman, and the power of their crystals joined together. As Aileen and I placed our magic into the circle, the web tightened, forcing our prey to cower.

"No!" Carman screeched. "Human scum!"

"Well, I never!" Mary Donnelly exclaimed.

"It's over," Sean said. "You can't hurt us anymore."

"We won't stand for it," Mairead added.

"No one messes with Derrydun," Beth said.

"No one at all!" Cheese Wheel Aoife cried.

Donkey *hee-hawed*, and Jack barked to add their support.

The light of our circle grew, whipping up a gale as Carman fought back with the Legacy she'd stolen. I felt Boone's power rise beside me, clear and crisp as it was when he'd grasped my ankle. We hadn't been enough to fight her then, but all of us together was just enough to bind her bitch ass in place.

"I have to close the doorway," Aileen said, her gaze meeting mine. "My spirit will bar the way, then you can end her. The athame is in my boot."

"No!" I exclaimed. If she did that, she would... I couldn't lose her again.

"It's the only way."

"No, you can't sacrifice yourself. Not again."

"*It's the only way,*" she repeated. "The loss of one life is better than the loss of millions. I know you wanted to save the witches magic, but it can't be done."

I desperately racked my brain for another solution. Boone was safe, his connection to his mother severed, but it would mean nothing if Carman crossed over into the fae realm. We had to kill or imprison her... Any of those would do.

My gaze caught Mairead's, and I had an epiphany. We had to give Carman a new home. One she couldn't get out of this time. One that would allow me to take back what she'd stolen.

"Can you hold her without me?" I asked.

"Skye..."

"*Can you or not?*"

"Not for long."

"I've got a better idea," I declared, hoping my crazy idea would save everyone, not just a few. "Stall her for as long as you can."

"Skye—"

"Trust me, Mum."

She choked, a tear falling from her eye. "That's the first time you've called me that."

"Third," I corrected her, breaking away from the circle. "Buy me ten minutes."

Aileen nodded, grasping Boone's hand. He stared at me, his wild hair blowing in all directions.

I blew him a kiss, then I was off.

My boots pounded on the path as I sprinted toward the village. The icy air burned my lungs, and my heart beat faster than it had ever beaten before. I was so not made for track and field. Short distances were my best friend. Why was the cottage so far away? I never did sign up for those mixed martial arts classes…

A branch whipped my face as I sped past, opening a cut on my cheek. Ignoring the sting, I pushed on, adrenaline fueling my flight. The coven was counting on me, so was the village. I'd vowed to protect them whether they knew it or not, and seeing them all standing there, all of them human, facing a thousand-year-old suped-up witch gave me the chills. I couldn't fail them now.

The cottage came into sight, and an otherworldly force I hoped was Siobhan urged me on. I leaped over the fence like an Olympic hurdler and barreled up the path, not even missing a step. I fumbled for my key, but dropped it, cursed, then used my Legacy to blast the lock open. The door crashed inward, cracking the plaster behind it. *Whoo, boy! It felt good to use my power openly for once.*

Skidding to a stop in front of Mairead's painting, I focused on the ruined tower house she'd painstakingly outlined with the tip of her littlest brush. *It was perfect.* Museum-worthy, even.

Just what I was looking for!

I practically tore the canvas from the wall and bounced back and forth down the hall until I was outside again. The painting was intact after my uncoordinated exit, so I ran toward the clearing, leaving the cottage door wide open and the picture balanced awkwardly against my head. It was massive, and the amount of work Mairead had put into it was on epic levels. *Man, I hoped she wouldn't be pissed.* Pfft! How could she be angry when her work was going to save the world?

That was if my plan worked. It *was* going to work. No ifs, ands, or buts. *It would work.*

Light filtered through the forest as I approached the

clearing, wind whipping the leaves into a frenzy. Debris whipped past my face as I ran down the path, the gust almost ripping the painting from my hands.

"*That's me paintin'!*" Mairead shrieked as I reappeared in the clearing.

Slipping back into the circle, I propped the canvas against me and held it steady with my free hand. I felt Boone and Aileen connect their Legacy to mine, and I was back in the game. *Time to suck that bitch into her prison.*

"You think you can trick me?" Carman cried. She was on her feet, pushing back against the villagers. "I have the Legacy of a thousand witches!"

"Yeah, fat lot of good that's doing," I drawled.

"We were always a match for one another. Two halves of a whole," Siobhan said through me. "You cannot overpower the united Crescent Legacy, Carman. Have you already forgotten in your lust for revenge?"

"Who's speakin'?" Maggie asked. "That's not Skye's voice."

I felt Siobhan's ghostly hand grasp my shoulder, and my Legacy flared. The golden light that bound Carman twisted around her, completely enveloping her body.

"*No!*" she shrieked, holding up her arms to shield herself. "You'll regret this, sister! I'll come back for you, and *you'll pay!*"

"I don't think so," I said, holding the painting steady as the witch was drawn into the image. "You'll never be free again, Carman."

A sucking sound filled the clearing as Carman's body circled the drain, her physical and spiritual essence flowing into the painting. She was ripped away from reality, twisting and turning, shrieking and calling us names, then she was gone.

The villagers let each other go with a collective sigh, the light from their crystals fading. The wind dropped completely, and the din created by the mini-tornado died down. Silence stretched out into the forest as we stood before the hawthorn.

Carman was gone.

The painting shuddered in my grasp, and I jumped. I almost expected her to break free as it shook and shook, but it held true.

"Freaky," Mairead said, staring at her masterpiece. "She's really in there?"

"Hey," Maggie said, turning toward the tree. "Is that music?"

"I hear it, too," Roy said.

"It sounds like a trumpet," Sean added.

I glanced at Boone, who nodded toward the hawthorn.

"Somethin's arrived," he said, taking the painting from me.

This time, I turned toward the light. The doorway was still open, and we still had to face what was on the other side. This didn't end with Carman. There was still more.

*Go…*Siobhan's spirit urged.

But I didn't know what was waiting for me. I imagined darkness and fire and a horde of grotesque fae waiting to devour my magic.

Come… This time, it wasn't Siobhan speaking to me. It was someone else.

Sucking in a sharp breath, I took a step toward the door. Who or what was inviting me in, there was no way of knowing, but I wasn't afraid. Calmness flowed through me as I let go of Aileen's hand.

As I walked toward the light, no one tried to stop me. I felt Boone's gaze on my back, but he didn't call out, either.

He knew what awaited me. He always did in a way, which was one of the things that infuriated me most about him.

We'd won the battle, but the next part of the story was mine and mine alone to tell.

When the time comes, open yourself…

I stepped through the doorway.

CHAPTER 20

S ummer.

Rays of golden light streamed through the canopy of a great tree, dappling over my tired shoulders. I looked up and found I was standing underneath a massive hawthorn, its shade stretching out across the greenest field I'd ever seen. Tiny white flowers dotted the mossy grass, and below the rise I stood upon, a forest stretched ever outward. A brilliant-blue butterfly flitted past my face, and the chirping of birds filled the sweet-smelling air.

What was this place? It was like a garden of Eden. It was a paradise, not a smoking ruin full of demons and monsters.

My gaze fell on a woman standing below me on the hill, and I froze.

She was small and lithe, her silver hair pinned up in elaborate curls and braids. Her skin shimmered like a pearl, creamy then tinted with translucent color as she moved. The silver and gold armor she wore was buffed to a high shine and reflected the sunlight like pure crystal.

She held a matching sword in one hand, whose hilt looked mysteriously familiar. *It's like the athame*, I thought.

She was definitely fae. I could feel magic everywhere. In the ground, in the sun, in the butterfly, even in her armor. She was alight with it.

Behind her stood a whole squadron of men and women, a hundred at least, armed and dangerous looking. They all held pointy swords, unsheathed and ready for combat. Beyond them, I could see the glimmer of silver hidden within the forest below. An army awaited, but was it friendly?

The woman, who appeared to be their leader, stepped forward when she saw me and slid her sword back into its scabbard. Good, the weapons were going away. That was a brilliant sign. At least they wouldn't skewer me without letting me speak first.

"You prevailed," the fae said, her voice soothing. She sounded almost child-like, but her eyes sparkled with age and wisdom.

"Who are you?" I asked, feeling like a complete loser in my torn and bloodied clothes. I was positive I had half the forest stuck in my hair. Wait, was there border protection here? What if I accidentally contaminated their world? *Oh, man…*

"They call me Aibell," she replied. "I am the Seelie Queen."

The Seelie Queen? I stood in awe, the beauty of her world nothing compared to her presence. Now I knew she was a queen, it explained a lot.

"You must be a Crescent Witch," she continued. "The one promised. I can feel your Legacy on the air."

"The one pr—" I shook my head. I was so done with prophecies and omens.

"Carman has been defeated?"

"She has." It felt good to say it aloud.

I glanced over her shoulder at the ranks of fae—men and women dressed in shimmering gold and silver armor —and understood. Our fear had been for nothing.

"You united the fae," I murmured.

"While you were fighting for your people, I was fighting for mine," Aibell said, gesturing to the soldiers behind her. "Two halves of a whole. Light and dark united. A thousand years of toil." The ranks sheathed their weapons and descended into a half-bow…all in perfect unison. "Night cannot exist without the day."

I couldn't believe it. No war had been waiting for us on the other side of the doorways. No death and destruction had come to claim us. Seelie and Unseelie had joined in perfect harmony for the first time in their history. The way had opened and with it came hope for peace. It wouldn't be easy, but it was a start.

"Carman would have brought destruction on both our worlds," Aibell explained when I hesitated. "With the power of all the human witches inside her, she would have been untouchable…even with the strength of the united fae behind me. When the portal opened once more, we did not know what would greet us. Carman's return was prophesized, but prophecies are often confused."

"So what the Crescents did…"

"Was a difficult choice but the only one that could have saved both our worlds."

Siobhan's sacrifice had been the right decision after all. Well, maybe not the right one, but the best of a bad bunch.

"Will you allow me?" Aibell gestured for my hands, and I nodded, dumbstruck by everything about her.

Her skin was smooth and cool to the touch, and when

her magic entwined with mine, it was as if the entire world opened up to me. My life flashed before my eyes, unveiling things I'd forgotten and others my mind had hidden from me. The dreams that had turned into nonsense were now clear, the visions I'd seen when I'd first used my magic to heal Boone after our fight with the craglorn—I'd almost died and the woman who'd sent me back…*Siobhan!* Even the rawness of Aileen's loss and the revelation that Boone was Carman's son were exposed. And my greatest shame…taking the Legacy of the Nightshade Witches.

A tear slid from my eye, moistening my cheek.

"I've seen your struggle," she murmured. "Don't be ashamed."

"I didn't want to hurt them…"

"You did what had to be done," Aibell said, squeezing my hands. "As all leaders must."

"I'm not a leader. I just…" I hesitated. "I did what had to be done. *Oh, man!*"

"You, Skye Williams… You did what no one else in your world had the courage to. I have not seen something so selfless since…"

"Siobhan."

The Seelie Queen nodded, her hair shimmering in the sunlight. "Siobhan."

"I admit, I'm kind of in awe right now." I glanced over her shoulder, taking in the world I'd been so afraid of Carman unleashing on my own.

"Humans often fear what they do not understand," Aibell said. "And often, so do the fae. Courage takes time."

"What now?" I asked. "I scarcely know what to do…"

"Do you speak for your people, Skye Williams?"

"The witches are divided," I replied. "But they've lived

in fear all their lives. Now Carman is gone…I suppose I should let them know."

"We can't undo a thousand years of separation, but we can help those who were lost," the Seelie Queen said.

"You can help the craglorn?"

Aibell nodded. "We can restore their health and hopefully, in time, their minds."

"Then we leave one doorway open. This one." I glanced over my shoulder toward the matching hawthorn that would guide me back to Derrydun. "Everyone gets a choice. The lost, the lonely, the sick, and the frail."

"That sounds like a wonderful idea, Skye Williams."

"What about Carman?"

Aibell tilted her head to the side.

"I imprisoned her in a painting," I explained. "She lives, but…"

"You don't know what to do with her?"

I nodded. "Yes, but I have an idea… I was able to take back the part of my Legacy a craglon took from me. Maybe…"

"You believe you can restore your people's lost Legacy?"

I nodded. "And strip Carman of hers."

"If it would please you, after you have completed your task, I shall take custody of the painting. Carman will no longer be your burden. Please allow the fae to guard her prison as a gesture of our gratitude."

I glanced at her and thought about it. Carman had wrought so much devastation on my world, raised crops and villages, murdered innocent witches, stole countless Legacies, and manipulated so many against one another. And she was a Crescent. That made her my responsibility.

"No," I finally said. "She was a Crescent Witch. She is

our responsibility. No matter what happens, she will be stripped of her power and never allowed to return. Believe me, she won't be comfortable."

"Then, all is as it must be."

"That's very trusting of you…"

"I've seen your soul, Skye Williams," she declared with a smile. "I know you speak the truth."

"Oh, goodie," I muttered.

Aibell laughed and swept her arm wide, her armor clinking. "On behalf of the fae, I welcome you, Skye Williams of the Crescent Witches, and all your people to our world. May we unite once more."

"Thank you," I murmured, gazing out over the vista. "The first step to a better future…"

"A fine first step, indeed."

**

Stepping through the portal underneath the hawthorn was a rush.

I burst out of the trunk with a yelp, almost falling flat on my ass.

"*Skye!*" Aileen flung her arms around me and squeezed.

Everyone was still assembled in the clearing, waiting to see what happened. Mairead and Boone held the painting between them, Roy and Sean breathed a sigh of relief, and Mary Donnelly hugged Donkey around the neck.

"Everything is fine," I said. "The fae…"

"Did they hurt you?" Aileen drew back and began checking all my extremities.

"Mum," I whined, twisting away.

"Just checkin'."

"The fae have united," I explained. "They were gathered on the other side ready to fight Carman."

Her mouth fell open.

"They were just like us. Waiting for an unknown terror to come and take them, but they found us instead. What a booby prize!"

"Far from it."

"Things are going to be okay," I murmured, looking over the extended family I'd found in Derrydun. They were staring at me in wonder, tears in their eyes. It was all a little overwhelming. "No war, no apocalypse. Just peace…and justice. It's over. *It's finally over.*"

"What was it like?" Mrs. Boyle asked, much to everyone's surprise.

"I'll tell you all about it at Molly McCreedy's," I said with a tired smile. "How about lunch tomorrow? I think we've all earned a rest."

"Hear! Hear!" Roy bellowed.

"Here's to Skye!" Sean shouted, fist pumping the air.

"Miracles do happen," I quipped, scratching my head. "Sean McKinnon likes me?"

"Don't press your luck," Maggie said with a wink. "All right you lot!" she called out to the villagers. "Let's go back to Derrydun! We've got a pile of snakes to sweep up."

As they made their way from the clearing, I was showered with more hugs and kisses than I could keep up with.

"We're still on for spring," Mary Donnelly whispered in my ear. "I never canceled anythin', just so you know."

One by one, they went until I was standing with Aileen, the painting, and an exhausted Boone. My mother muttered something and took the painting to the other side of the clearing to give us a moment. It was a long time coming.

Boone's gaze was fixed on the ground, his shoulders slumped. The battle had been hard, but his journey had been the most difficult of all. I stood before him, unsure of what to say. After everything we'd been through, it was difficult to know where to begin.

"You have matters to attend to," he murmured. "And so do I."

"But…"

Knowing Dub and Dother were still lying on the road in the center of the village made my heart twist. I couldn't leave Boone to bury his brothers on his own. No matter what they'd done, they were still his flesh and blood. I had to help him.

"I must do this on me own," he said, combing a hand through my hair.

"Are you sure you're not telepathic as well?" I asked, tilting my head to the side.

"Just…" He sighed, and let me go.

I nodded and brushed my thumb against the engagement ring on my finger.

"If you need me," I began.

"I will find you," he replied. "I always do."

I was frozen to the spot as I watched him go, a strange melancholy blooming in my heart.

"Let him be," Aileen said, coming to stand beside me. "He'll come back when he's ready."

"You were right about the spirit." I glanced away from Boone's receding form, unable to watch him walk away again. "It was Siobhan. Carman's sister."

"Carman's sister? Oh, *cac*…"

Now that we were alone, we sat on a fallen log overlooking the hawthorn, and I explained it all to her. The vision, Carman's story, what had happened to Boone's father, Finn. I left nothing out, and she didn't interrupt, letting me get it all out.

"I was going to marry my cousin," I said, my heart more confused than ever. "Siobhan's blood is mine. That's why the ritual needed to be performed on me. Siobhan's blood was the key to breaking the curse she put on Carman."

"You're right about that, but Boone isn't your cousin, Skye," Aileen said. "He is half Crescent, but he never shared blood with you."

"How…"

"In the beginning, all witches were one, and when the first covens were formed, they took their bloodlines with them. The Crescents were of many different strands a thousand years ago. The Crescent Legacy was passed on through spirit and still is, though we are the only bloodline remaining. That's why Siobhan's blood was mixed with yours even though she was from a different family. When you touched the hawthorn, and it showed you those visions, it allowed her spirit to attach itself to yours. It's been growing ever since."

"When I hit my head… Those dreams…"

"I don't know what that's about, but I suspect it was her spirit trying to come forth and give you what you needed to face her sister."

"Where is she now?" I held out my hands and stared at them like they would reveal all the lost secrets of the witches. "I can't feel her at all. Not that I ever did, but…"

"Her spirit likely lives on beside yours," Aileen explained. "Her task has been completed, and she can either stay or return to the hawthorn and watch over the doorways with the other ancestors. That's a conversation you and her will have to have. When you're ready."

I rubbed my tired eyes, smearing my mascara.

"It's over, Skye," she said, wrapping her arm around

my waist. "The witches are finally free, and it's all because of you."

"I don't feel comfortable being called a savior," I said, gazing upon the ancient hawthorn.

"A reluctant heroine," Aileen quipped. "Those are the best kind, you know."

CHAPTER 21

Staring out my bedroom window, I was surprised to see Derrydun didn't look any different.

After yesterday's commotion, I was sure there would be smoke on the horizon, but the view was the same as it had always been. Green, misty, and vibrant despite the gloomy sky.

Stepping into my boots, I donned my jacket and pulled out the beanie and gloves Boone had given me at Christmas. I had a lot to do today, and even though we'd won the war, it didn't mean Mother Nature had turned up the heat.

On the way out, I checked in on our houseguest.

Mairead's painting of Derrydun was propped up against the wall in the living room, surrounded by crystals and a bowl with a stick of sage before it. The room reeked, which meant Aileen had been in here obsessively cleansing. I didn't blame her. I would probably be doing the same if she wasn't here.

As if it sensed my presence, the painting shuddered

then lay still. *Still as mad as a bee in a jar, I see.* I thought about shaking it but turned around and went outside.

My return to the ancient hawthorn was a great deal calmer than it had been last night. When I stepped off the path and into the clearing, I was startled to see the state of the furniture or so to speak.

Bark and branches were strewn everywhere, and the trees around the edges looked rather sad. We'd really done a number on this place, but it wouldn't be a battlefield without a few scars. There were still a few snakes lurking around the village, but thankfully, they'd lost their spark and dropped dead once Carman was sucked into the painting. Mary Donnelly was currently spearheading a working bee back on the main road to round the stragglers up.

"It was quite the scene," Siobhan said. "Human and witch together."

"Don't forget the equine and canine."

Siobhan stood beside me, a little transparent around the edges. I wasn't surprised to find she resembled Carman but the spitting image? That was a new one. When she'd called her sister, I imagined a few years difference between the pair, not a few minutes. She was Carman's identical twin. That was another story for another day, it seemed.

"So, that's what you look like," I mused. "Two halves of a whole. I get what you meant now."

"Disappointed?" She laughed, her eyes crinkling at the corners.

As she turned, she aged before my eyes. Where Carman had done everything in her power to stay young, Siobhan had remained in Derrydun and allowed nature to do what it willed.

I shook my head. "Not at all. You were with me this whole time… I just wondered."

"I'm sorry that you had to face my sister," Siobhan said. "I wish things could've gone differently. For you and her sons."

I turned toward the hawthorn and gazed up at her branches. The berries were starting to fall.

"Boone…" I began with a sigh. "I assume he has his father's heart, unlike his brothers. I never sensed anything but kindness in him."

"Finn was kind, as is Dain, that is true. Carman was always quick to anger, and I hoped his love would teach her a different way. Bein' the best never seemed to be enough for her. When he died, any light she had in her heart faded. Unfortunately, it never returned."

"The world or bust," I mused. "Power corrupts…"

Siobhan nodded. "Sometimes."

I glanced at her, wondering what she meant.

"I can't think of a better witch to lead the Crescents into the future," she continued. "Skye Williams, you have our blessin'."

"Wow. The ancestors are blessing me with their magical juju?" I laughed and shook my head. "Took them long enough."

"Be careful," Siobhan said with a chuckle. "Your 'sass,' as you call it, might get you into trouble."

My laugh echoed around the clearing. "Oh, man, it feels good to be alive today."

"And so, I must leave you to enjoy it."

"It's over now," I murmured. "All is as it should be."

"Thank you, Skye." Her ghostly hand brushed against my cheek. "You had the courage to do what I could not."

A cool breeze fluttered against my skin, and when I turned, Siobhan was gone.

**

Father O'Donegal was sweeping out his church when I emerged from the forest.

All the doors were open, and he was manning a straw broom, his blazer draped over the back of a pew, and his shirt sleeves rolled up to his elbows. A tan streak roared past the pulpit as his tabby cat pounced and played with a severed snake tail.

"Ah, Skye," he said when he saw me. "Good mornin' to ye."

"Good morning, Father. The snakes didn't make too much mess, I hope."

"They certainly didn't mind slitherin' into the house of God," he muttered, swiping the broom at a little green critter.

I chuckled and turned toward the church grounds.

"Thank you," he said behind me. "You showed real courage yesterday."

Glancing back, I smiled.

"He's in the cemetery," he added after a moment.

"Thanks."

My boots crunched on gravel as I rounded the side of the church, the mossy lichen covered Celtic crosses and headstones standing tall in the yard. They all bore familiar family names like McKinnon, Donnelly, McKinney, and Byrne. I wondered how many were Crescents and where Siobhan's resting place might be. Likely someplace deep in the forest.

When I stepped around the rear of St. Brigid's, I saw him immediately. Even if my eyes were closed, I would've found Boone. Now his Legacy had been revealed, it was almost as familiar to me as mine. He was part of the Crescent Coven, after all. *Man, my boyfriend was a thousand years old, give or take. He really was a silver fox!*

He was sitting on the end of Aileen's empty grave, overlooking two fresh mounds. *His brothers.* A shovel was propped up against a neighboring headstone, and I knew Boone had been out here all night.

He'd changed into his usual getup at some stage—a checkered red and black shirt, jeans, and boots. His coat was folded in a heap on the ground next to him, and his curled hair was wild and sticking up all over the place. It looked good, though. His hair. Always did.

I crossed the cemetery and stood beside him, waiting to be invited. When he shuffled over, I sat. Our legs pressed together, and it was warm and familiar. Just as it should be.

"Sean came by and helped for a while," he murmured after a moment.

"That was good of him."

"Aye…"

"I just returned your aunt to the hawthorn," I said.

He grunted, scuffing his boot against the ground.

"I'm sorry about your brothers…"

He shrugged, looking exhausted. "They were corrupted a long time ago. This endin' seemed…inevitable."

I didn't know what to say to that, so I added, "I'm sorry about your dad, too."

"I was too young to remember him," he replied. "Mother always said he was murdered to start a war between the witches and the fae, but Dother told me it had been a rogue Unseelie that took his life. The wrong place, and the wrong time. An accident of circumstance. It's hard to know who to believe."

It had certainly begun in a gray area. Carman lusted for power even before Finn had died, and her heartbreak gave her the excuse to take advantage. Boone knew it, and so did I. We didn't need to dwell on such things. Not anymore.

"When you came to Derrydun…" I began.

"I'd broken free," he replied. "She cursed me, but when I was able to get into Ireland, she altered the spell. Probably hoped that one day I would help her break the curse keepin' her out. I guess she didn't count on me fallin' for the last Crescent."

"Help? More like use," I muttered.

"She was me mother, but that never meant she had me loyalty," he said. "She locked away me memories before I could escape but couldn't spell me into obedience."

"You did escape," I murmured, threading my fingers through his. "You came here."

"I almost didn't make it."

I picked up his hand and threaded my fingers through his.

"There," I said. "Proof you're here, and we're together."

I felt him tense, his magic rippling through our joined hands, then he untangled himself and glanced away. *Awkward.*

"Are we related?" I asked, trying not to be so butthurt about it. "Is that…"

Boone lowered his head. "No. At least, I don't think so."

"Good. Because getting married would've been illegal."

"I suppose we are distantly related."

"Aileen said the coven was large back then," I

explained. "There wasn't one pure bloodline. The Crescent Legacy was passed through spirit, not blood. The hawthorns are what binds it all together."

"You have her sister's blood, Skye."

"Not like you think. I was the last, so Siobhan's spirit came to me because her power was needed. That's all. Those weird purple monkey, alligator, typewriter dreams were her spirit trying to meld with mine. It sent my powers into overdrive." I smiled and looked out over Derrydun. "So our kids aren't going to have two heads."

"Our kids?"

"There's nothing in my oven, so don't get too excited. I don't even know if I want to pop out any mini-humans. Thinking about pushing something that big out of my vagina isn't exactly my idea of fun."

"What about the coven? You and Aileen are the last…"

"Boone, the time of the Crescent Witches is over. We've righted the wrongs, made peace with the fae, expelled all the evil in Ireland… It's time for the forgotten to reclaim the world. The lost fae will be able to go home, the witches can come out of hiding, and everyone will be able to let go of their fear and live the lives they've always wanted. I have to stand back and allow them to take back their own Legacy."

"So we can take a break?"

"Yeah. Our work here is done." I laughed and nodded, liking the sound of that. "Hopefully, one day, the witches will see what happened here and not hate the Crescents so much. We'll invite them to come to Derrydun to see if we can restore their power, and go from there." Maybe the Nightshade Witches would be able to earn their magic back, too. That was a comforting thought in light of everything that had happened.

"What about us?" he asked uncertainly. "I mean… The last time we spoke, it wasn't very nice."

"I'm sorry," I replied. "I shouldn't have pushed you away like that, but I meant what I said yesterday. I love you, Boone. I always will. Nothing will ever change that."

He twisted to face me, his eyes wide with hope. "You still want to marry me?"

I held up my hand and showed him the ring. "I never took it off."

He let out a whoosh of air, grasped my face, and kissed me. Wrapping my arms around his middle, I held him close, pouring all the love I felt for him into our embrace.

"We're still on for spring, you know," I murmured against his lips. "Mary didn't cancel."

"Well…I better find a suit."

"Don't borrow clothes from Sean McKinnon ever again, by the way. Go to Sligo where there are proper shops."

Boone grinned and glanced up at the sky where the web protecting the village—the one Aileen and I had created—and the natural glow of the hawthorns lay dormant.

"I will," he said with a laugh. "I'm free to go wherever I choose now, after all."

"Well, don't go too far. We've got a party to go to!"

CHAPTER 22

A LITTLE BIT MORE…

I felt the last of Carman's stolen magic emerge from the painting and flow through my body. The unfamiliar magic skipped along my skin and dove into the woman whose hand I held.

"There," I said. "Do you feel any better?"

She'd given her name as Amanda, a witch from Blarney in County Cork. Twenty years old, worked in the woolen mills near the castle and had been caught unawares one evening after a night out with friends. Carman had taken her Legacy, and with it, her trust for anything living.

"Yes," she said, staring at me in wonder. "I can feel me magic again."

Seeing her Legacy flow back into her body made me feel proud to be able to use the gifts the Crescents had given me to restore her belief in the world.

"Take a break," Aileen said, placing her hand on my shoulder. "Go enjoy the festival."

"That was the last one," I said, glancing up at the hawthorn as Amanda rejoined her family. They embraced and chattered happily as she tested out her magic. "There's no more Legacy left."

"Then let me do this last part," she replied. "You've done so much, Skye. Besides, you have to take it easy."

"Thanks, Mum." I rubbed my eyes and rose to my feet, my back aching and a strange craving for tomato sauce sandwiches tickling my tastebuds.

Making my way back to the village, I thought over everything that had happened in the last six months. After the battle with Carman, fae crossed into Ireland and assisted those too wild or too frail to return on their own. Craglorn passed through the portal where healers were on standby, ready to help them recover. It was a confronting sight for the villagers, but they'd seen weirder things. Sean McKinnon and Maggie Ashlyn starting a romance was one of them.

Humans also returned from across the realms. They were the descendants of those that had been left behind, but after so long living among the fae, many decided to go back.

When we began spreading the word about the possibility of returning lost Legacies, witches had started appearing. One or two, to begin with, then whole covens rolled up when they'd heard my efforts had been successful. They came from as far as County Donegal in the north, to Kerry and Cork in the south. Their covens were large and small, their talents as varied as the colors of their Legacies. I heard their stories, and they heard mine, and it seemed the Crescents were back in the good books.

And Boone with magic that wasn't shapeshifter related was weird. It explained his magical tongue and silver animal shapes, at least.

The riotous sound of a traditional Irish folk song

echoed through the edges of the forest as I emerged. Turning down the main street, I smiled and breathed in the scent of candied apples, fish and chips from a witch-driven van that had traveled all the way up from Dingle, and popcorn from a stall selling fairground snacks.

Derrydun had put on a Lughnasadh celebration to welcome visitors from all over Ireland and beyond. It was a Gaelic festival that marked the beginning of the harvest season on the last Sunday of July, so the village had been decorated with garlands of hawthorn leaves, Virginia creeper, and twists of rushes and corn stalks. It was also called Garland Sunday, and people climbed to the summit of Croagh Patrick on a pilgrimage to honor Saint Patrick who, in the year four hundred and forty-one, spent forty days fasting on the mountain. Or so Boone told me.

All the stores were open, and tables laden with local produce and crafts were set up all along the main street. Molly McCreedy's was in full swing, as was Mary's Teahouse. Seeing the handprinted sign out the front of Mrs. Boyle's spruiking it as a bed-and-breakfast, I had to have a little chuckle.

Even Fergus had set up at his usual spot beside Mary's Teahouse. Donkey and Jack posed for photos as he weaved his crosses of St. Brigid for the visiting witches. His tipping pot was overflowing with gold coins, and he looked pleased as punch with all the attention.

A makeshift stage sat in the car park where the Tralee Witches were performing a lively rendition of *Whiskey in the Jar*. They were more like a traveling band than a coven, with two fiddlers, a guitarist, a tin whistler, and a drummer. Though when they played, I was sure I felt a little magic among the notes. Talk about supercharged *craic*!

Wandering among the stalls, I smiled and greeted people as I went. Witches, fae, and humans alike.

Phee yapped excitedly as Roy dangled a sausage in front of her nose, but she didn't clamp her jaws around the tasty morsel until he'd given the command. Sean and Maggie walked hand in hand, and he teased her with a stick wound with bright pink fairy floss. Mrs. Boyle was handing out flowers to a group of little girls instead of chasing them with her broom. Cheese Wheel Aoife was rushed off her feet in her shop, and next door in Irish Moon, Natalie—the overexcited witch we'd hired to help us out over the summer—was zapping crystals left, right, and center with the trusty laser scanner.

Stopping by a display of landscape paintings, I shook my head. Mairead had been busy since the battle, whipping up canvases small and large. Everyone who'd come to reclaim their Legacy had wanted to see the painting that held Carman and meet its artist. The result was a mob around her Garland Sunday stall, a tangle of selfie sticks, an overflowing cash box, and commissions to last her the next ten years at least. Everyone wanted something painted by the artist whose work now held the most dangerous witch in history. Talk about an epic career change.

All was well in Derrydun…and all over Ireland.

"Are you Skye?"

I turned to find a trio of girls staring up at me with eyes as big as moons.

"That's me," I replied.

"Can we take a selfie with you?" the elder of the group asked eagerly.

I laughed and gestured for them to squeeze in. I made a peace sign as she snapped a few pictures of me and her friends, and when they were done, they scurried off, giggling excitedly as they went.

"I see you've been busy while I've been away," a voice said behind me. "You've gone and got yourself a fan club!"

Spinning on my heel, I jabbed a finger at Robert O'Keefe. "*Where have you been?*"

"You never needed me help, Skye," he said with a chuckle. "Besides, I had a pot of gold to keep warm."

"I knew it!" I jumped from foot to foot. "I told Boone you were a leprechaun."

"Not so loud." He hushed me, glancing around nervously.

"Leave him be, Skye. He's a rascal but a loveable one."

I turned as Aileen appeared, looking a little frazzled around the edges. When I gave her a look, she nodded.

"It's done," she said. "Carman's Legacy has been stripped, and the painting has been handed over to Aibell and the fae."

Man, I was glad we'd changed our minds about taking ownership of Carman's prison. With a bun in the oven, I had more than enough to worry about without her sticking around.

"That's good to hear," Robert O'Keefe declared. "Many good wishes to you both." He glanced at my stomach. "Ah…*four*."

"*Four?*" I screeched.

"Err… Sorry?"

I spun on my heel as Boone appeared through the hubbub of the festival, looking sheepish.

"Twins!" I screeched. Circling my arms around my swollen belly, I scowled at him. "We discussed this!"

"I think we ought to escape," Aileen said to Robert. "The honeymoon is about to be over."

"We can't fight nature," Boone said with a grimace as they moved away. "I can't help it if I'm potent."

Married four months, and knocked up on my wedding night… I couldn't even think about my growing baby house without breaking out into hives.

I slapped him on the arm and groaned. "I'm going to have to push two out at the same time now. Thanks a lot!"

"I'm pretty sure they come out one at a time," he quipped, earning himself another slap. "It's a blessin', Skye. After everythin' the Crescents have been through, we have a future now."

"I know," I said, resting my head on his shoulder. "It's just that I know how much of a handful they're going to be. I was a bloody terror, and I didn't have my magic!"

"We'll be all right," he murmured, wrapping his arms around me. "They'll have an entire village dotin' on them."

"You're always right," I said. "It's infuriating."

He chuckled and kissed the top of my head. "I love you, Skye."

"I love you, too."

The Crescent Legacy would live on, not only in our children and the hawthorns but in everyone here. Our story would become song, history, legend, and myth. That was how these things worked, after all.

The hawthorn in the middle of the road was laden with ornaments and envelopes filled with memories of the lost and wishes for the future. But that was not what I was looking at. Underneath its branches stood a young girl with wild curly blonde hair, who had probably turned sixteen by now. She reached up and hung an envelope, then wiped at her eyes.

"What are you lookin' at?" Boone asked.

"I'll be back," I murmured, untangling myself from his grasp.

Waddling across the street, I stood underneath the branches of the hawthorn and ran my fingers over all the memories. So many witches.

The girl glanced up at me, tensing when she saw who'd come to speak to her.

"I'm sorry about your sister," I said. "And I'm sorry about taking your Legacy, Christine."

The Nightshade Witch's cheeks turned red, and she glanced at my fattening stomach. "You're…"

"A leprechaun told me I'm having twins," I declared, then made a face when I realized how absurd that sounded. "Are you enjoying the festival?"

She glanced away while her fingers worried the hem of her T-shirt.

I waited, knowing she was too afraid to ask.

"I was hopin'…" she began awkwardly.

"You came to ask me for your Legacy."

Christine nodded, trying to hide behind her hair.

"What about your mum?"

"After Lucy died, she said she didn't want anythin' to do with magic ever again." She scuffed her toe on the ground. "She doesn't know I'm here."

"It's a long way from Galway," I commented.

She shrugged. "I suppose."

The longer I studied her, the more I got the feeling that she wasn't quite like the other Nightshade Witches. She was young, eager, and had the courage to come all the way to Derrydun and face the Crescents. She had guts, especially after the ritual. I didn't blame Lucy for what she did. She was brought up in a household full of prejudice and tainted with her ancestor's use of dark magic, but

Christine was different. Maybe it wasn't too late for her to change her future and break away from the past hurts her coven wrought on mine. Perhaps we could help one another step into this new world. She was part of a new generation of witches, after all.

"You know what? I have just the thing in mind." I placed my hand on her shoulder and nodded toward Irish Moon. "How about a summer internship? I could use the extra pair of hands…and I might be able to teach you a few things."

The teenager's eyes lit up.

"Now, it won't be easy," I went on.

"I know," she said. "I know you won't give me back me magic right away, but I'll try me best. I promise."

I smiled, her enthusiasm warming my heart…or that might just be heartburn. Either way, there was a big dollop of hope in there.

Wrapping my arm around her shoulder, I guided her away from the hawthorn and into the midst of Derrydun.

"C'mon," I said. "I've got a few people I'd like to introduce you to…"

The End.

Continue the Crescent Witch Chronicles with, **Crescent Rogue***!*
It's time for Boone to tell his story…

OTHER BOOKS IN THE CRESCENT WITCH CHRONICLES

series is complete!

The Crescent Witch Chronicles is a series stuffed full of Irish charm, myth, and mayhem. Come on an adventure fraught with danger and romance…and the ultimate battle to save magic before it's gone forever.

Crescent Calling #1
Crescent Prophecy #2
Crescent Legacy #3
Crescent Rogue #4

Find out more at: www.nicolertaylorwrites.com

ABOUT NICOLE

Nicole R. Taylor is an Australian Urban Fantasy author.

She lives in the western suburbs of Melbourne dreaming up nail biting stories featuring sassy witches, duplicitous vampires, hunky shapeshifters, and devious monsters.

She likes chocolate, cat memes, and video games.

When she's not writing, she likes to think of what she's writing next.

Follow Nicole Online:

Website: www.nicolertaylorwrites.com
Facebook: facebook.com/nrtaylorwrites
Newsletter: www.nicolertaylorwrites.com/newsletter
Email: nicole.this.is@gmail.com

Find out more at: NicoleRTaylorWrites.com

See what titles are FREE at: Nicole's Free Reads